DEAR CLARE

Three days, seventeen hours and twelve minutes ago, I became a vegetarian.

At our school, they showed my class a film about factory farming. At the end of it, the whole class voted to become vegetarians at once. We all boycotted the school dinner and just ate the chips. One of the Dinner Ladies, Mrs Sampson, said, 'Every year it's the same. They won't last the week.'

I have changed to packed lunch now and steer clear of school dinner because Mrs Sampson does not play fair and waves her frankfurters tantalisingly and shouts, 'Who's for hot dogs, Class 3?' Which is quite annoying to a learner vegetarian . . .

The collected correspondence of Ms Anna Pitts, aged 13.

Dear Clare,
My Ex Best Friend

Ursula Jones

Illustrated
by Rebecca Elgar

KNIGHT BOOKS
Hodder and Stoughton

Text copyright © Ursula Jones
1991

Illustrations copyright ©
Rebecca Elgar 1991

First published in Great Britain
in 1991 by Knight Books

Typeset by Medcalf Type Ltd,
Bicester, Oxon. Printed and bound in
Great Britain for Hodder and
Stoughton Paperbacks, a division of
Hodder and Stoughton Ltd., Mill Road,
Dunton Green, Sevenoaks, Kent
TN13 2YA (Editorial Office: 47
Bedford Square, London WC1B 3DP)
by Cox & Wyman Ltd., Reading, Berks.

British Library C.I.P.

Jones, Ursula
Dear Clare, my ex-best friend.
I. Title
823[J]

ISBN 0–340–54390–6

82A, Lucien Road,
London, SW17,
England,
The Planet

October 11th

Dear Clare,

What's Australia like? Do you go surfing every day after school? Nothing has happened in England since you left except the usual tons and tons more pollution.

I have tried to ring the prime minister about it but they said he was not in. Even when I told them I was thirteen they still said he was out. You usually get put through to top people when you tell them your age because they reckon you'll be a push-over if it comes to an argument. I'll have to send a letter instead which is bad news because it's pocket money on a stamp and phoning is free because Mum pays.

Sorry I'm late keeping our pact to write to each other till we are grown-up ladies. Mum says we should say women, well she would if she read my letters to my friends but she doesn't. Mum cannot help being old fashioned. It is her age.

The people who moved into your ex-house last week are newly-weds. They stay at home all day and keep their curtains closed which makes me think some tragedy is blighting their bliss but Sis says more likely they are watching television.

Your first letter hasn't got here yet. Mum says you've only been gone two weeks but Sis and I make it five weeks, two days, eleven hours and sixteen minutes. That's 381,180.89 more tonnes of sulphur dioxide emitted from Britain since you went and if Sis had switched the calculator off when she last used it so the battery hadn't just gone on the blink I could tell you how many litres of acid rain had fallen on the whole world since you went too.

Please write to your Australian prime minister and tell her/him how worried you are by such statistics. I am trying to get Sis to write to ours as well but she is convinced that if she does, they will send MI5 round to our house.

It was Sis's birthday yesterday. She gets excited. She had a ballerina and eleven pink candles on the cake. When it came to blowing them out, she was sick instead.

We couldn't eat the cake.

Mum had to put one of the guest's dresses in the washer. After they had all gone, we found she had taken her present to Sis back home with her. Quelle crudité!

Sis cried.

Mum said it was a good job though because Sis is too young for blusher.

When are you old enough? Thirteen whole years and I still have to stop off at Boots every day for a quick go with the tester. I really have to whisk it over my face now too because the assistants lie in wait to catch me and make scornful remarks about the last of the big spenders.

No wonder I always get to school lopsided.

I rubbed so hard to tissue it off on the way home that Simon, our new lodger that we have so we can pay Mum's mortgage, said to me when I got in 'Hello Brickface.'

I nearly died.

Simon has pale, blond hair and steady, blue eyes and the hairs on his jaw are golden red. He is seventeen. He smiles like George Michael. He says he's a Yuppy. He smells stunning, specially when he has been playing squash. I told him I wanted to be an actress and he smiled like George Michael till I had to sit down and hold my homework in front of my face.

I got Sis to find out if he has a girlfriend and the answer is NO!!! I am on a diet. I went faint in geography.

During the news tonight, Mum said, well she shouted more, 'We ought to get out of this dump of a greed divided society and go to Australia like the Hannocks have.'

My heart swelled when Simon answered, 'It's a fair division. Those who provide the in-put deserve the pay-out.'

'Hear, hear,' Sis murmured staring fervently at him and Simon *smiled* at her and she smiled at Simon.

I will never trust my sister again.

'Yes, let's emigrate, Mum,' I said bitingly, to show Simon I would not care if there was a million miles between him and me. 'We can't,' she said. 'Not while the Piranha is alive.'

Mum is taking us to visit the Piranha this weekend.

With love from your friend in England,
Anna Pitts

82A, Lucien Road,
London, SW17,
England,
The Planet

October 11th

Dear Prime Minister,

My mother told me that one day you will get your just deserts. I am very sorry about this.

Speaking of deserts, wouldn't it be terrible if the whole of our beautiful planet became one? And it will if you do not stop pouring acid rain on to it from British chimneys.

Our lodger says you are just what Great Britain needs so cheer up, nobody is all bad.

Yours sincerely,
Anna Pitts
Aged 13

82A, Lucien Road,
London, SW17,
England,
The Planet

October 16th

Dear Clare,

It's Sunday night now and we've only just got back from Gran's.

Quelle outing!

We had a puncture on the motorway and we

8

couldn't undo the nuts on the wheel to change it, not even when Sis, me, and Mum all jumped on the thing that undoes them together. None of the men driving past dared stop to help in case they raped us.

Mum's AA membership was two years out of date.

Sis cried.

The police came.

We were three hours late for the Piranha's and she'd thrown the dinner in the freezer. Mum said, 'I'm exhausted,' and the Piranha said, 'It's your own fault, Daughter, lumbering yourself with not one but two fatherless children.'

Sis cried.

Mum sent us out for a walk.

We were starving but Sis had brought her birthday present money with her because she is scared of burglars so we spent it on fish and chips. Bang went my diet.

Typical Mum.

Then Sis cried because we had spent all her birthday money.

Then it rained.

The spikes in my hair came unwaxed.

A boy in a bus shelter said, 'Hello, Curly.' And belched. I could have died.

I longed for some blusher to put on. And on Sis.

We tried to get through to Child Line, but the phones were vandalised.

When we got back from our forced walk, the Piranha and Mum were drinking gin. The Piranha was laughing and Mum was halfway through a box

9

of tissues so now she's caught a cold and I bet she gives it to me.

The Piranha said, 'We are going to live in the country. Your mother is going to leave her job with the old crocks,' (Mum's job at the community centre, she meant) 'and we are going to make full use, at last, of your mother's talents.'

All the way home I thought about the country. These are my thoughts: the country is a perilous place.

It is typical of my parent to compel me to live alongside lager louts and pesticides and shooting parties and other such dangers without asking me how I feel about it, but that is not the worst.

Clare, I dread moving.

How can I say goodbye to Simon? Oh Simon, Simon. Nobody cares if I die of crying.

Mum's talents are news to me.

With love from your friend in England

Anna Pitts

82A, Lucien Road,
London, SW17,
England,
The Planet

October 18th

Dear Clare,

I have my heart's desire – a photograph of Simon. Mum took photographs at Sis's party and he is on one of them. I have cut him out and he is under my pillow.

A miracle has happened in hockey. Remember Joanne Blakely, who is deaf? Well, she fell over when Anita the Great tackled her, I think because she did not hear Anita the Great running up behind her. That's really deaf. Next thing, and we all saw even if Miss Jolly didn't, Anita cracked Joanne over the head with her hockey stick but afterwards nobody said anything about it to Miss Jolly because Joanne jumped up in consternation shouting, 'I can hear, I can hear!'

And she could.

Miss Jolly whispered in her ear to test it and Joanne heard the whisper. Quelle miracle!

Joanne went home early to show her mum and dad she needn't go to Special School now so my side lost the match 2-6.

Today, all the girls in the class took Joanne down to McDonald's for a burger to celebrate her new found faculty but we would not take Anita the Great even though she had been God's tool in the miracle. That will teach her to foul.

No more talk of moving to the country. Phew! Phew!

The Prime Minister made a speech to say no one will be able to make any money out of the planet if we don't look after it so my letter has certainly got everyone worried.

I am making up a play about Acid Rain. Sis won't be a dead tree though. Sometimes I could kill her.

With love from your friend in England,
Anna Pitts

82A, Lucien Road,
London, SW17,
England,
The Planet

October 26th

Dear Clare,

Mum and the Piranha are wasting all the half-term driving Sis and me round and round the country looking for a house to buy.

For today's trip, I wore my black mini with my bomber jacket. The Piranha said my mini was too short. Mum said a mini had to be short to qualify as a mini.

The Piranha said, 'Like mother, like daughter.' Which was really mean of her. Mum is not anything like the Piranha even though they both wear their skirts too long.

All the houses we look at are old-fashioned. One of them was even made of stone like a church. Believe it or not, it wasn't finished off properly. There was a bit in the front where you could still see all beams and stuff showing through the walls.

Mum said that it was probably Elizabethan. It is amazing what people will try and sell you, isn't it?

It was once a butcher's shop. I am thinking of becoming a vegetarian.

The Piranha said the butcher's shop would be too far away from Mum's clients. So now Mum's got clients as well as talent.

That Piranha lives in a dream world.

Your first letter still hasn't come. Mum says it's in a bottleneck caused by our district postal strike.

I am writing to the local paper today so I shall take it round to them by hand.

Guess who asked me for your address today when he delivered our newspaper this morning. Baz Goodbody. Expect a Christmas card! His voice has broken. The only boy in the class whose has. Wimp Walters says his has but it hasn't.

Isn't it wonderful the way the supermarkets are keeping the dolphins out of the tinned tuna nets? I have decided to re-join Greenpeace.

When I told Simon about Greenpeace, he said he had just enrolled in the Society For The Advancement Of Dog Eating In The UK.

Simon's laugh does not really match him. It is a little bit squeaky.

Have you Started yet? About .3 of the girls in our class have Started and the rest are still waiting to Start. Anita the Great Started in the first year Juniors!

I keep sensing I have Started. I pretended to the Piranha five times today that she had to stop the car for me to be excused but it was really to look and see if I had Started but so far, no luck.

I will try and get a photo of Simon for you too.
With love from your friend in England,
Anna Pitts
P.S. The Piranha has just phoned Mum to say I ought to be sent to the doctor about my waterworks. A.P.

To:-
The Editor,
South West Chronicle,
London, SW17

October 26th

Dear Sir,
I disagree with A.L. Bosworth when he wrote last week to say your readers should quit worrying about global pollution and put their own house in order by taking tough action against the dog dirt in our park. We are.
We are cutting down five acres of rain forest every minute and taking life-giving oxygen away from the world and so we will all die. Then there will be no parks and no dogs to do dirt in them and no people to write to the papers about it even if they write on recycled paper.
Yours faithfully,
Anna Pitts
Aged 13

82A, Lucien Road,
London, SW17,
England,
The Planet

October 29th

Dear Clare,
On no account write any more to the above

address. We are moving to the house of stone. Our new address will be –

The Old Butcher's,
Leachfield,
Gloucestershire,
England,
The Planet. KEEP IT OR KILL IT?

Mum is leaving her occupational therapy job at the old folks community centre.

Sis is crying.

Simon has applied to join the Navy.

He told Mum he is fed up with YTS and wants a wife in every port. I shut myself in the bathroom to cry and cry about this but they all kept banging to go to the toilet.

Mum has made an appointment with the doctor for me about my waterworks.

Sis stopped crying to say it was a good job we were moving to the Butchery because it has two toilets. She is too young to know about love. I love Simon so much my stomach aches with it.

I hope and pray your first letter gets here before we move in eight weeks time.

I must stop now and pack.

With love from your friend in England,
Anna Pitts

To:-
The Editor,
South West Chronicle,
London, SW17

October 30th

Dear Sir,

I disagree with A.L. Bosworth that I have been brain washed by Trendy Lefties and the Kennel Club about dog dirt in the park.

No, I do not have babies yet who will roll on the dirt during picnics but if people go on cutting down five acres of rain forest every minute, I won't be having any babies at all. Nobody will be.

Yours faithfully,
Anna Pitts
Aged 13

82A, Lucien Road,
London, SW17,
England,
The Planet

October 30th

Dear Clare,

Yesterday, at the Halloween disco, Anita the Great asked me where we were moving to and I told her about the butcher's house of stone and Mum's talents and clients.

This morning, Anita told Sarah, my second best

friend (you are still my first), not to sit next to me in Orientation and Community studies and she didn't. Nobody sat next to me all day.

Sis waited at the gates to go home with me this afternoon. She was crying and said Anita the Great had put it all round the school that Mum was going to the country to become a scrubber. I asked her what a scrubber was and she said it was a lowly sort of cleaning lady.

I believe Sis is wrong about that so I guess she was crying from snobbery or just habit.

Do you know what a scrubber is? Please let me know by return of post if you do.

October 30th 10 p.m.

Don't worry about the scrubber information. I asked Simon and he told me.

It is a Slag.

Well, I must close now.

Simon has a big blackhead on the side of his nose.

With love from your friend in England,
Anna Pitts
P.S. No need to mention the Scrubber bit to your mum. Please give her my love. A.P.

17

82A, Lucien Road,
London, SW17,
England,
The Planet

November 2nd 10 a.m.

Dear Clare,
I have dropped my slogan KEEP IT OR KILL
IT? Simon says faced with the cost of keeping it,
most people would opt to put the boot into the
planet.

I was sick in the night so I'm not at school.
Mum's out at work at the old folks community
centre.

I was sick with worry about Mum going to be
a scrubber. At first I could not believe it because
she is so old and is always shouting about women
being free. Did she mean all the time that they ought
to charge?

Surely she can see what a fool she will look, she
does not have the right clothes for it. Also it is a
very un-hygienic profession and fraught with pitfalls
when you think of the commercials for AIDS. Mum
could be wiped out and Sis and me orphaned.
Typical Mum.

November 2nd, 1 p.m.
I was sick again then a lady came to the front
door. She is coming again when Mum gets back
from work. She asked if I was Sis and I told her
no, Anna. I think she is probably a social worker.
Obviously she has heard about Mum's new career
and come to take Sis and me into care.

I am the sickest I've been so far. It's the worry.

Once I asked Mum why the Piranha is called the Piranha. She said it was because she has had so many husbands. She is a man eater.

Like mother, like daughter.

With love from your friend in England,
Anna Pitts

82A, Lucien Road,
London, SW17,
England,
The Planet

November 5th

Dear Clare,

The lady came back when Mum was home. She came running into the living room to take us into care.

I was sitting on the sofa reading *Mizz* with a bowl in my lap in case I was sick again and with my fingers in my ears to keep out the noises Sis was making practising on her recorder for the school Christmas carol concert.

I really, really want to stay with Mum whatever her misdeeds and not be sent to live in the council home. I pushed my bowl under the sofa and said, 'I do not like the tower of any place.'

That's what the little Prince of Wales says to Richard III when the cruel king is going to incarcerate him and his brother but the king did them in nonetheless.

Mum frowned funnily but she is not classically

19

minded and the lady said to Sis, 'Oh my darling, you are so like him.' Then she hugged Sis and I heard the recorder go clunk against Sis's front teeth. Then the lady said, 'I'm your Granny, darling.'

Sis just stood there rubbing her front teeth and Mum said, 'It's your dad's mother.'

I was so relieved, I began to laugh. She is a really classy dresser. Not like the Piranha.

Sis cried.

Then Sis hugged the lady back and the lady hugged Sis back and then I hugged her too and said, 'Welcome, Granny,' and she said, 'Well, actually, dear, I'm your sister's granny, not yours.'

I could have died.

Sis and I have got two dads. One each.

Typical Mum.

I went into the kitchen and because I had left my bowl under the sofa, I had to be sick outside the back door just as Simon was coming in from a hard day's slog at his YTS job. He said watching people puke was good experience for the navy and he really did stay and watch.

I could have died.

While Sis is out shopping with her Gran this morning, I am going to have a private talk with Mum and plead with her to give up her new career as a scrubber and to convert our car to lead-free petrol.

November 5th, 4:23 p.m.

I told Mum straight that if she wanted me to stop vomiting with worry, she would have to give up her selfish plan to go to the country to be a scrubber. She was really angry so I did not get round to the lead-free petrol.

Mum called me a silly little drama queen, which was hurtful even though to a budding actress this should have been a compliment.

She asked how a daughter of hers could have a mind like the *Sun* but she did not give me a chance to explain how.

I made her a coffee.

She asked didn't I ever listen.

In our house you don't get the option to do anything else.

She said as I hadn't been sick for over twenty-four hours, wasn't it more likely to be the bug that half the school has gone down with and not worry that had made me ill.

Nobody agrees with me that I have feelings.

Then she said in her special, bringing-up-children voice, Sis and me having two dads didn't make her a prostitute.

Mum can't half get hold of the wrong end of the stick sometimes.

Then she said how Sis and me were the product of Great Love. I have heard all that bit before so I said it was time for my doctor's appointment.

Mum can be very outspoken at times.

She left her coffee which is a waste now they have frozen Child Benefit.

It turns out that Mum was at Art School when she was young and we are going to the country so that she can stencil, whatever that is. She is going to do it to people's walls and floors and furniture. She is fully confident that they will pay her for it.

I met Anita the Great in the doctor's waiting room. She has the sick bug. I fixed to fight her in

21

the dinner hour when she comes back to school for calling Mum a scrubber.

Clare, a terrible thing has happened while I was out. My photo of Simon has gone from under my pillow.

Sis came back with her new Gran and lots of new clothes. Now her new Gran has taken her into town for a bonfire night fireworks display.

Simon and me and Mum are going to the council fireworks. Sis tried to come too but Mum said New Gran would be disappointed if Sis didn't go with her. So off she went in all the new gear but she looked really angry.

Bliss, bliss. Simon all to myself for the whole evening.

With love from your friend in England,
Anna Pitts
P.S. Give my love to your dad and mum, Mr and Mrs Hannock. A.P.

82A, Lucien Road,
London, SW17,
England,
The Planet

November 6th

Dear Clare,
Simon brought a girl called Rachel to the council bonfire night celebrations. She is doing the same YTS job with him. She is sixteen. She is size ten and 175 centimetres tall. Unlike me, she is blonde.

22

Sorry. It's November 8th now.

Thanks to some sneaking creep, Miss Jolly broke up my fight with Anita the Great before the cow could kill me.

I wish Miss Jolly hadn't interfered because I want to be dead. I love Simon so much but he has no eyes for me and so I am thinking of Ending It All.

This will probably be my last letter to you.

With love from your friend in England,

Anna Pitts

P.S. Give my love to your dad, Mr Hannock, and to your mum. A.P.

82A, Lucien Road,
London, SW17,
England,
The Planet

November 9th

Dear Clare,

On no account write to me at The Old Butcher's, Leachfield, Glos., England, The Planet, YOU NEED IT, IT DOESN'T NEED YOU. The man who owns it is selling it to someone else for £2,000 more than we can give him.

Mum is in hysterics because she has sold our house to Mr and Mrs Webster and their new baby so now we will be homeless and I will have to give up the idea of suicide because I am the eldest.

In her dolour, Mum has drunk all seven of the cups of coffee I have made her.

So, no more country and Old Butcher's for us. Phew! Phew!

Please write to the President of the USA. Say something like –

Dear Mr President,
Our Planet is in Peril. Please put a stop to chlorofluorocarbons in air cooling systems that puncture the ozone layer. We may be cool today but tomorrow we will roast in the terrible Greenhouse Effect. And the earth will become like Hell. So who wants two Hells? I know you can do it. Please do it quickly. I am thirteen. Yours sincerely . . .

That's what I said. You can copy mine if you like. make a few little alterations then he will not notice the letters are identical.

Keep in the bit about being thirteen. If you don't, he will think you are a cranky grown-up and his secretary will reply.

With love from your friend in England,
Anna Pitts

To:-
The Editor,
South West Chronicle,
London, SW17

November 9th

Dear Sir,
My mother has told me not to write in reply to

24

A.L. Bosworth any more because it is becoming too quarrelsome but before I sign off, I hope A.L. Bosworth will agree to shake hands on the dog dirt once and for all.

Yours faithfully,
Anna Pitts
Age 13

82A, Lucien Road,
London, SW17,
England,
The Planet

November 10th

Dear Clare,

I have found my photograph of Simon under my sister's pillow.

I hit her.

Would you believe it! Sis's new Gran is a make-up lady for the television and knows all the Stars. She was really encouraging when I told her I wanted to be an actress. She said the most surprising people become actresses and that contact lenses come in very attractive colours these days but I told her I am hoping to grow out of my glasses.

Sis's father, New Gran's son, lives in Los Angeles and is a Stunt Man. When Mum heard that she remarked, 'You can say that again.'

Quelle crudité!

New Gran has spent many years tracing Sis. I hope it was worth the bother.

November 10th, after tea

I have just asked Mum for further details of the other dad. Mine.

She always says he is an art student whenever I ask. He's been an art student ever since I can remember so I don't rate his chances of making it to an artist if it's taking him this long to learn.

Mum was still having hysterics about the Old Butcher's when I brought up the subject and screamed, 'What a time to ask!'

When is the right time to ask about your dad? I know he was called John but nearly everybody is. Perhaps Mum wouldn't answer because he is someone shameful like Mr Cecil Parkinson with the oily hair.

November 10th, 10 p.m.

In revenge for being hit, Sis has told Simon I keep his photo under my pillow.

I can't face him. Ever.

I am in bed. I won't dare go down to breakfast. I wish I was anorexic.

With love from your friend in England,
Anna Pitts

P.S. Give my love to your dad, Mr Hannock, and to Mrs Hannock as well, of course. A.P.

82A, Lucien Road,
London, SW17,
England,
The Planet,

November 11th

Dear Clare,
It's really expensive avoiding Simon. Because of
the photograph incident, I set my alarm for six and
left the house this morning before Simon was up.
Nobody else was up either.

It was dark and the street lamps were still on so
it felt exactly like the middle of the night. I checked
my watch in case it was. I'm not experienced with
my alarm because you don't need one in our house.
Mum always wakes us up clanking around in the
kitchen, extinguishing the toast and shouting at the
radio.

Then I met Baz Goodbody on his paper round
so I knew it was truly the morning and he let me
deliver all his papers to get me warm while he
practised skid stops on his bike.

I was starving. One bar of Kit Kat
from the corner shop: 20p

After school, I went to Pizzaland and
bought some tea with a bit of the money
from my Christmas shopping savings: £3.15

I rang Mum up from a box to say I
was at Sarah's doing a joint project and
wouldn't be home until 9.30:   10p

Then I went to the pictures. It was
Richard Gere but I enjoyed it: £3.20

I bought some chips to take home for

27

supper. I climbed through the kitchen window to remain unobserved. I need not have bothered, they were watching the News at Ten. I could hear Mum abusing the announcer. I ate the chips in my bedroom. I could hardly chew for yawning. Anyway, they were tepid.   50p

TOTAL £7.15

Sorry, it's November 18th now

I have had this really brill idea. I'm going blonde, blonde, blonde. I have bought the stuff to do it with and tomorrow is the Big Day. The Blonding of Anna Pitts.

I kept on with avoiding Simon though it burnt money. I set out at dawn next day. But it was harder because it was Saturday and no school. After I'd tried on all the clothes in the high street and tested seven new blushers, I had a hamburger and french fries and a raspberry yoghurt drink: £3.50.

Then I went to an early showing of the Richard Gere film but it was a different man selling tickets and he said I was under fifteen and couldn't go in by myself. I said I was fifteen but short for my years and he said, 'Clear off, Four Eyes, you are holding up the queue.'

I went to the toilets and put on some of my brand new blusher. I have decided to come out about blusher. So. Another 99p.

When I am a big star, I will fly over to that cinema on Concorde with Richard Gere and I will give everyone there my autograph except that man, no matter how he begs and pleads. Or maybe we'll come in a balloon. It's less polluting and slightly more sensational.

I was in bed by four o'clock in the afternoon and my Christmas money has gone down by half.

Sunday was worse because Baz does not deliver the Sunday papers. A cross old woman in fake fur ear muffs does it instead.

Guess who I met though. Anita the Great. She was wearing a pale blue shiny dress with many frills and her Walkman. Except for the Walkman, she looked like a bridesmaid. She was going to church. I was really cold by then and as there was nothing better to do, I said I'd go too.

We stopped at my house for my best coat because Anita said my anorak was too casual for the Lord. Nobody was awake – the sluggards! Simon sleeps downstairs in what was the dining-room when proper people lived here. I crept past his room with my broken heart banging.

In church, I played the tambourine and sang along with the choir. The hymns were fantastically good and some of the people there bopped to them. After that, the preacher gave a really interesting talk about Love Thy Neighbour, and I gave £5 of my Christmas present savings money to the collection. I decided I must have more spiritual feelings towards Simon and I went home to try it.

Mum was reading the papers in bed. I took her a cup of coffee and asked her, dead casual, if Simon was up yet.

She said, 'Anna, you live in a world of your own. Surely you've noticed that Simon has been away since last Friday. He has gone for a week's holiday in Sevenoaks.'

I did not mean them to, but the tears came out of my eyes. Of course, I could not tell Mum why. She gave me the rest of her coffee and made room for me next to her and did not say a single word about my blusher. Then I taught her one of the hymns I had learnt in church. We sang it till Sis woke up and came in to see what was wrong.

Saturday 19th November

Clare, Clare. I've done my hair. I did it while everybody was out buying another house. It looks wonderful. A golden mane. Much blonder than that Rachel of Simon's. I'll send you a photo.

Saturday 19th November, 6:30 p.m.

Mum came back without a house. She opened the front door and screamed when she saw me. The Piranha took me into the living room and gave me a really serious talk about how upset my mother was at the moment and how I must behave responsibly. I told her I was because I had given up suicide for Mum's sake but she said not to be melodramatic.

New Gran came in with some new red shorts for Sis. She looked at my hair and said, 'You poor child, that is going to take weeks to get rid of.'

The Piranha rang a hairdresser. I am to miss Monday morning school and go to have my hair cut off.

Sunday 20th November, 4 p.m.

Simon is back from Sevenoaks. He says my hair looks great. They can stuff their hair cut.

Monday 21st November

I have had my hair cut really short, like Annie Lennox.

By the way, Simon has been staying with Rachel at Sevenoaks.

With love from your friend in England,
Anna Pitts

82A, Lucien Road,
London, SW17,
England,
The Planet

November 25th

Dear Clare,

Please write to your prime minister at once. Complain bitterly to her/him that every single letter I have sent to you in Sydney has been returned to 82A, Lucien Road, London, England, The Planet, Y.N.I. I.D.N.Y., strapped together with rubber bands and with Return to Sender stamped all over them. Thankfully, they have not been tampered with. Phew! Phew!

No wonder you never answered them. You never got them. The Australian post office is playing fast and loose and denies you live at 75, Ryan Street, Sydney, NSW 2040, Australia, The Planet, Y.N.I. I.D.N.Y.

But why am I writing this letter? There is nowhere to send it.

9.30 p.m.

On no account write to complain to your prime minister about the Australian post office. Mum has confessed all at tea.

She said Sarah, my second (you are still my first) best friend's dad had a birthday card from your parents. I was thirsting for further information but just then the radio started playing 'Lucy In The Sky With Diamonds.'

That is a Beetles song.

I know that because Mum went into one of those raves old people have about the Beetles. And then they always finish up in a kind of trance so Sis and me thought we had lost her for the evening.

I switched off the radio to plug Mum back into the twentieth century. And she said the birthday card said you had all moved house.

I asked Mum why she hadn't informed me and she said, 'Anna, you live in a world of your own. I told you the Hannocks had moved on to Narrowmine.' I asked her when she had told me. She replied that she'd no idea I had written all these letters to you.

She said she was proud I had written so many letters.

I can read my parent like a book. This was a mega butter up. What is there to be proud of? Mum would get really annoyed if I said I was proud every time she wrote a letter.

Gnawed by guilt, Mum has said she will pay the cost of sending this parcel of letters to you in Narrowmine.

What an interesting place it sounds, Narrowmine. I have been looking for it on the map but I expect it will turn up any minute.

Just in case you think the parcel is an early Christmas present and are disappointed, I have put in a photo of Sis and me. It is before my hair so it is not bang up to date.

Sis is on at me to put out my light. It is going in her eyes, she says. I said to put her pillow over her face but gently to avoid snuffing it. She said she knew all along that you had moved to Narrowmine.

With love from your friend in England,
Anna Pitts

P.S. Sorry about the photo. It got nail polish remover on it. Hastily, I wiped it off with my sheet but alas, it had dissolved poor Sis. A.P.

82A, Lucien Road,
London, SW17,
England,
The Planet

Y.N.I
I.D.N.Y.

November 26th

Dear Clare,

Mum and the Piranha are out looking for a house to buy. Sis is at dancing class. Simon is at the library finding a book about the navy so I have the place to myself.

There are no leaves left on the trees in our road. They are all on the pavement. The Piranha says it is a danger to OAPs and they should privatise the road sweepers.

New Gran pays for Sis's dance class. Sis teaches me the steps when she comes home so I can be a

Dancing as well as Acting Star. In return I help her with her homework.

The Websters and their new baby are moving into our house in four weeks and two days time on December 29th so then we will be without a home. Mum's so hysterical with our situation, she has forgotten all about Christmas so I expect that will be a dead loss.

Typical Mum.

Speaking of losses, as the Old Year wanes, I am reflecting on other losses. In the last eleven weeks and six days I have lost my best friend (to Australia), Simon (to Rachel), my hair, half a sister (because Sis and me have separate dads) and the planet has lost 83 species. I have had a near miss with a new Gran and am stuck with the Unknown Student and the Piranha for family. And Mum.

I suppose she is my mum. Maybe she adopted me. If that is the case, I am seriously short of relatives.

I must stop now and make the Christmas pudding as a treat for everyone and because there's no way Mum will. You will be having your Christmas dinner on the beach. All Australians do, watched over by swarthy Life Guards and Koala bears, happy in the knowledge they are a protected species.

Seven and a half minutes later
A man has phoned to say the Old Butcher's is for sale again at the original price and does Mum want it. I am sad to say, it would be really wrong not to give Mum the message.

34

Thirty-five minutes later

Baz Goodbody called up and asked me round to his house this afternoon to listen to records. I must stop now and have a bath and wash my hair and choose my blusher and decide what to wear.

With love from your friend in England,
Anna Pitts

82A, Lucien Road,
London, SW17,
England,
The Planet

November 27th

Dear Clare,

I have been up since 6 a.m. finishing my play about Acid Rain so Baz can read it. His records are brilliant and not one New Kids hit. Phew! Phew!

We had a great afternoon and we kissed. I have not done it before. Have you? At first my glasses dug into Baz's face but then I took them off and we had a second try which was better. I think there are probably rules about the breathing though, like in swimming.

Please let me know if you have any further information on that.

Baz's mum came in from work, she is a taxi driver, and gave us a cup of tea and I went home.

Mum and the Piranha had just got back and there was a terrible row because –

(a) the kitchen was full of half-mixed Christmas pudding so they couldn't make a cup of tea.
(b) I had borrowed Sis's new red shorts to go to Baz's in without asking. The ones New Gran gave her.
(c) I had broken the zip.

Sis cried.

Mum ranted.

The Piranha started to give me a serious talk and I have to admit, I threw the pudding mixture at her.

It was awful. It landed all over her mink.

The Piranha drove off home in her Rover like an iceberg. She would not even stop to be wiped down.

Mum hit me although it is against her beliefs. Then she sniffed a lot. I thought with tears of remorse – but no. She accused me of nicking her duty free *Diorissimo* that your mum gave her when you all came back from Majorca.

It was true.

New Gran came in and said I was a teenage hooligan and had they all seen the state I'd left the bathroom in. Mum said, 'Shut up you misguided old bag.'

It was awful.

Mum bawled on and on at New Gran. All stuff about showering Sis with too many presents and sibling resentment, whatever that is. The bow on New Gran's silk blouse waggled with the heaviness of her breathing.

Sis said. 'How can you ever have too many presents?' And New Gran said in a panting voice, 'Blood is thicker than water.' And I made a little joke about blood baths to calm everybody down and

Mum went berserk.

Somehow Mum's got this idea the mess I made of the bathroom was New Gran's fault.

Typical Mum.

She comes up with the weirdest theories. And she can't really believe it or she would have sent New Gran to clean the bathroom and not me.

When I'd finished it, I had another bath as it seemed a pity to waste all the lovely new cleanness. Quite by accident, Mum's *Diorissimo* fell into it but I managed to rescue a dribble at the bottom of the bottle.

New Gran is not speaking to Mum.

Neither am I.

After all, I could not help it about the *Diorissimo* and as I said to her, who wants to smear themselves with deers' glands anyway? Because that is what perfume is, but Mum could not see it.

Sis can't teach me this Saturday's new dance steps because she is not speaking to me.

The Piranha is not speaking since the Pudding and Coat incident.

Nobody is speaking.

I am thinking of advertising for my long-lost relatives.

The dictionary says a sibling is one of two or more persons having one or NORMALLY BOTH PARENTS IN COMMON. Ha ha.

With love from your friend in England,
Anna Pitts

P.S. Simon says the Australians eat kangaroo. If you catch one doing it, I think you should take action. A.P.

82A, Lucien Road,
London, SW17,
England,
The Planet

November 29th

Dear Clare,

I am really disgusted and thinking of writing to the Ombudsman.

I rang the *Standard* with my advertisement for a relation. I got as far as 'Loving school girl seeks her long lost granddad – ' I thought I would start with a granddad because we have an overdose of grans in our family, and then work up to my dad. Anyway, the woman on the other end said really nastily, 'We don't take that kind of advertisement, thank you very much.' And she cut me off.

Quelle crudité!

So I am no nearer some relatives.

Baz really likes my play about Acid Rain. It is called *Killer Drops*. We are going to do it at school for Christmas. First rehearsal is at our house tomorrow.

Anita the Great has agreed to take the part of The Planet Earth. Joanne Blakely, who was deaf, will be The Guardian of a Stricken Pine Forest, somewhere in Norway, and Sis, because she is taking dancing lessons, is the Wicked A.R.

Anita the Great's brother might help with the music. He is a disc jockey. There is a really good fight at the end between Green Buttons (Baz) and the Bad Fairy fossil fuel, Pollutant Moll (me).

Baz and I have kissed again. It is nice.

I am so embarrassed. My mum is so embarrassing. We were right in the middle of our first rehearsal of *Killer Drops*, when Mum comes storming into the living room. 'Anna,' she said, 'Why didn't you tell me the Old Butcher's was back on the market?'

It was only then I remembered the telephone message. I said I was sorry and Mum went mad.

Isn't it funny the way they do that? Even though you have just stated you are sorry?

Baz said she went Ape. Do they use that expression in Australia?

The rehearsal stopped and my friends tried to leave. Only a rhino or a tragically paralysed person would have stayed. But Mum wouldn't let them go. She kept saying, 'Please don't leave, dears, I'm not going to spoil your fun but . . .' And then going into orbit about how I was selfish and stupid and self-centred and how I'd lost the Old Butcher's for us and finally she said that if I thought more about my family and less about the damn planet, yes *damn* planet, I'd be a better person and we'd all have somewhere to live.

We had 82A, Lucien Road to live in until she decided to move.

After Mum had gone raving into the kitchen, there was a really tense silence. We could hear Mum beating up the kettle in there. Anita the Great said perhaps Mum ought to see a shrink, like her mum does.

Sis cried.

Joanne Blakely, who was deaf, said she'd never

heard anything like Mum before but then she has not heard a lot.

I was so embarrassed, I thought I was going to faint but it was just my glasses misting up.

We all went round to Baz's and Mr Goodbody gave us some beer to drink that he'd made in their airing cupboard but it needed sugar for my taste.

Mr Goodbody has offered to coach Baz and me in our fight. He goes to Karate lessons every Tuesday night with Mrs Goodbody.

Have you got a granddad? Maybe you would like me to contact him. He might be missing you all now you have gone to Australia.

With love from your friend in England,
    Anna Pitts

To:-
The Prime Minister,
The Prime Minister's Office,
PO Box 8001 PET,
0030 OSLO 1,
Norway,
The Planet

December 3rd

Dear Sir or Madam,

I am very sorry that we in Britain are killing all your beautiful fir forests with a brutal cloud of fossil fuel pollution.

If I was in charge of this country, I would put

a stop to it at once but alas I am not old enough and anyway, I am going to be an actress not a prime minister.

What beats me is why you go on sending us one of your rare, unblemished trees every Christmas to put in Trafalgar Square.

This year, why don't you send a letter instead? It needn't be a war-like missive – just explain politely how we have struck down your trees and you can no longer spare us one for our Yuletide Merry Making, and that is sure to alert the people to their shameful deeds.

Wishing you a very Happy Christmas.

Yours faithfully,

Anna Pitts

Aged 13

To:-
The Prime Minister,
10, Downing Street,
London,
England,
The Planet

Cherish it **OR** Perish with it.

December 4th

Dear Prime Minister,

Thank you for the speech you made in reply to my letter of October 11th. And for your resolve to improve.

I hope you don't mind me saying this but I think it is really un-Christmassy of us to kill the

Norwegians' fir forests with pollution and then make them send us one of their last living trees.

Mum says it is something to do with World War 2 but I say let bygones be bygones.

At this rate, in exactly fifty years time, there will not be any forests left in Europe.

I know this is hard for you and your ministers to worry about because you will all have had to face The Great Mystery by then (like the forests) but I will only be 63 years old. I will probably be a Dame and living in modest luxury in Hollywood.

Or will I?

Will anyone or anything be anywhere?

Will we have perished along with our planet.

Brr! What a chilling thought! So I hope that will convince you to go for it and save the world.

Yours sincerely,

Anna Pitts

Aged 13

The Old Butcher's,
Leachfield,
Gloucestershire,
England,
The Planet

January 6th

Dear Clare,

Mum and me went to the January sales and bought me some BRAS! My first.

They are very pretty. Much the prettiest of all

my clothes really and after you take it off, it itches. I am 'A' Cup. That's the smallest – but you ain't seen nothing yet.

This place is huge and cold except for the Piranha's flat on most of the first floor which is warm and snug because she has got carpets and curtains and wallpaper and fires and radiators. We have not.

Mum says stone flags and bare, polished boards are more artistic and will impress the clients and we are to wear sweaters.

Sis and me each have a big freezing room of our own in the attic now. Mum is too busy stencilling and stuff to notice we haven't any curtains that fit. I have to hang my summer clothes in my window for modesty.

Mum is scumbling a wall at the moment which means smearing it in a tasteful fashion. The stencilling is really, really, beautiful but it is very easy to make mistakes. Mum has quickly learnt some amazing swear words. We moved in two days ago.

The mail is being re-directed so now the Christmas rush is over, I am expecting your first reply to my letter parcel any day.

We had a stunning Christmas. We couldn't move out of Lucien Road on the 27th December as planned because everybody in England goes on holiday for a fortnight round about then and that includes removal men. When we told the Websters and their new baby this, they cut up really rough so we had to move ourselves out.

The Piranha hired a huge, self-drive van and Mum hired Stan and Rick who are two very nice

43

members of the black economy. Rachel and Simon helped too but they weren't much use as they were always lying down on the beds. New Gran kept standing them up again and saying, 'Cool it,' in a joke voice.

When we arrived here, the electricity was off. The man at the Electricity Board who could turn it on was taking a fortnight's holiday too. Mum became quite ratty.

We unloaded the van, which took hours and then Mum gave Stan and Rick a carrier bag full of bank notes and they drove the van away. We all stood there in the cold and the dark and pondered the situation.

Sis cried.

Then Sis said she wanted to go home.

Then we all cried.

Next thing, the Piranha and New Gran clubbed together and paid for us to go to a hotel. Have you been to a hotel? There was a Christmas treasure hunt and clean towels every day and many-coursed meals. Quelle après Yule!

Killer Drops was a huge HIT. Anita the Great lost an embarrassing piece of her costume in the first half but she swiftly ran into the wings and Wimp Walters, our stage manager, tied his T-shirt on her. He has sisters.

Anita's brother filled in the pause with really professional music and after that nothing else went wrong and everybody remembered their words.

Baz's and my fight was terrific. Anita the Great's brother did bone crunching noises and Mr Goodbody had mixed up some excellent blood which gushed out of my mouth.

44

A girl in the fifth form had to lie down in the staff room because of it.

Baz and me have split up. He took Joanne Blakely, who was deaf, to Santa's Grotto. Personally, I cannot think of a more boring place to go.

I have had a letter from Washington DC to say the President is busy but when he is not he will write to me about the planet. Quelle brush off!

New school on Monday. At least it will be warm.
With love from your friend in England,
Anna Pitts
P.S. I looked in the phone book for your granddad and got through to Mr G. Hannock but he said he wasn't your granddad. Then I tried Mr J. Hannock but he wasn't him either. Mrs L. Hannock answered when I rang Mr L. Hannock and told me that Mr L. Hannock had died recently so I hope that one wasn't him. There weren't any more Hannocks in the book. A.P.

The Old Butcher's,
Leachfield,
Gloucestershire,
England,
The Planet

January 10th

Dear Mrs Hannock,
Thank you for your Christmas card to us which arrived today. The Piranha says the Australian post office should be privatised immediately under Prince

Charles so the letters would get through more briskly and give HRH something useful to do while he waits to reign instead of idling about chatting to his vegetables.

I agree. Doesn't the picture of the Sydney opera house look like a bunch of bananas. Mum says that is modern beauty. But you know Mum.

Thank you for your complimentary remarks about the number of letters I've sent to Clare. Tell her when she gets back from summer camp not to worry as I know there is a lot of reading to get through in that parcel before she can reply.

I'd forgotten it is her summer holidays. As I watch the rain drops coursing down the darkened window panes of the Old Butcher's, I picture her outward-bound outback wandering amongst the prickly pears and eucalyptus trees for four whole lucky weeks.

What a nice photo you sent of Mr Hannock and Clare by your pool with Kenny, from next door. Yes, he is a nice looking boy, isn't he. Australia appears very hot and comfortable.

Well, I must close now.

Happy New Year.

Anna

The Old Butcher's,
Leachfield,
Gloucestershire,
England,
The Planet

January 10th

Dear Clare,

Beaucoup de commiserations about Kenny who lives next door. Cross fingers you will meet a really dreamy boy at summer camp to make up for him.

The Piranha says Australia is full of rabbits and convicts which must be inconvenient when you are living under canvas. Then she let me have a sip of her gin and tonic to cheer me up. It didn't. It tastes a bit like toilette water. Don't get me wrong. I mean the sort you buy on the perfume counter at the chemist.

Then I returned to my own quarters for tea because man cannot live by gin alone. The only sign of tea was Mum in a reverie over a saucepan of baked beans. She snapped out of it though to say gin caused miscarriages.

Sis cried.

To comfort her and show I was not at risk, Mum gave her a whole anatomy lesson – diagrams, the lot – she really rubbed my immaturity in. Then we had the Junior Encyclopaedia out, and then revision of the Facts of Life plus the usual Great Love angle.

Then Sis said she was crying because I had had gin and she hadn't.

Mum said to eat up but by then the beans were

all cooked to the bottom of the saucepan and the toast had got lost.

Over our Jacob's cream crackers, Mum said Australia was full of sheep so it sounds pretty crowded one way or another.

Today, when I told the Piranha there were sheep as well as escaped rabbits and convicts in Australia, she said, 'Who has been filling your head with nonsense about Australia and convicts, Anna?'

Is that what is called a trick question?

With love from your friend in England,

Anna Pitts

The Old Butcher's,
Leachfield,
Gloucestershire,
England,
The Planet

January 20th

Dear Clare,

Three days, seventeen hours and twelve minutes ago, I became a vegetarian.

It is all right except Mum keeps forgetting. Yesterday, when I undid my packed lunch, she had given me all ham sandwiches so I could only eat the outsides. I gave the ham to the school goat. It ate it but it looked at me most sadly afterwards so I think it is secretly a closet vegetarian.

Mum is the only one on my side about being a vegetarian even though she absent mindedly tried to give me chile con carne today. She says it is very high principled of me. The Piranha said, 'Principles, my eye, Daughter. It is cheaper to feed a vegetarian and you know it.' And she added darkly that I would be carried off with anaemia and Mum would be done for neglect. Mum said she was more likely to be sent down for debt the way trade was going.

Comme toujours, New Gran came to stay for the weekend and she said me being a vegetarian was a phase and fattening.

Sis doesn't give an opinion. She has stopped talking about anything except ponies since we moved to the country.

Sis has made friends with a girl called Daisy. Daisy has a pony which she sometimes lets Sis have a go on but mostly Sis just polishes it after Daisy has finished riding it and Sis comes home all smelly.

Daisy doesn't go to our school. She is a weekly boarder at a nearby castle which is really a school in disguise. It stands in sumptuous grounds and you have to pay to go and get taught there.

At our school, they showed my class a film about factory farming. It is too horrible to describe and anyway, I missed a lot of it because in the most terrible bits I took my glasses off so I could not see. Two of the boys had to stand outside for air.

At the end of it, the whole class voted to become vegetarians at once and I said I would write us a musical about factory farming but Butch Hills said, 'Back to the drawing board, Big Head. It has been done already by a Mr George Orwell.'

I don't know why he is called Butch because he is really quite short. His face reminds me a little bit of a bowl of muesli and he sits at the back with Gerald Tappering. Gerald Tappering has outgrown his strength which makes him walk in a wavery manner.

We all boycotted the school dinner and just ate the chips. One of the Dinner Ladies, Mrs Sampson, said, 'Every year it's the same. They won't last the week.'

Quelle crudité!

I have changed to packed lunch now and steer clear of school dinner because Mrs Sampson does not play fair and waves her frankfurters tantalisingly and shouts, 'Who's for hot dogs, Class 3?' Which is quite annoying to a learner vegetarian.

With love from your friend in England,
Anna Pitts

The Old Butcher's,
Leachfield,
Gloucestershire,
England,
The Planet

January 24th

Dear Clare,

Sis really shames me, hogging away at beef burgers in school dinner. Egged on by Mrs Sampson. Mrs Sampson says Sis will grow into a beautiful lady. But then, everyone is entitled to their opinion.

My whole class is still vegetarian except for Robin Westlow who has had to change back to meat because his father says he will pulverise him if he does not, but Mr Westlow is a stockman and makes his living from this cruelty.

Last night, I asked Sis if she would like me to fry her up a pony burger.

Sis cried.

Mum said 'Anna, people won't thank you for it if you push your principles down their throats,.'

'Ponies, not principles,' I quipped. But Mum did not get it.

Mum had another letter from the bank manager this morning and that always makes her snappy so I ate my pasta without mentioning that I have had pasta for tea five days in a row.

Going to school in the country is really weird. There is no public transport so we are all taken in special school buses. Everybody is white which is quite eerie.

51

Our uniform is maroon so you can imagine how hard it is to find a blusher that will tone in but Shereen, my new friend, is very helpful with advice.

Shereen's mum lets her wear all the make-up she can buy which is a lot because she has a Saturday job collecting eggs and earns money. She is trying to get me a job there too.

I have an unwaged job. When I come home from school, I have to sit in the old butcher's shop which Mum calls the Gallery, and mind it while she gets the supper and no one comes in. Ever.

Sometimes Mr Bull, the reporter, drops by but then Mum always comes out of the kitchen to talk to him and so I have to go and make the supper instead.

Mr Bull wrote an article for the local paper about our shop when it opened and he visits us quite often to see how it's going. My friend Shereen's mother says Mr Bull has three grown-up children that he abandoned when they were little but Mum said, 'So what's new?' And asked him to supper.

The Piranha came down from her flat to complain about something but we never found out what because when she saw Mr Bull, she went all smiley and stayed to supper too even though Mum gave the Piranha one of her frowns.

The Piranha smiled all through supper and said funny things that even made Sis and me laugh. She was hilarious about Mum's cooking. I think Mum must have had another letter from the bank manager though because she never laughed once and seemed to be brooding on something.

It's my guess the Piranha has man-eating designs

on Mr Bull which is a bit shocking in the elderly. It could mean I'd have a granddad though but I would have to share him with Sis and I would prefer to have one of my own.

Sis hasn't got a granddad because New Gran does not have a husband. She told us she has lost him. When I suggested the Salvation Army could find him with their missing persons bureau, New Gran said that that was not funny.

Mr Bull brought a bottle of wine to the supper party and I fell asleep over my homework. When I woke up I had dribbled on my history and was filled with strangely sad thoughts. These are my thoughts: the country is a no-no for a budding actress.

That's all. So it's more of a thought than thoughts.

There is no school play until Christmas and it's only a pageant, whatever that is.

Daisy says every girl at her school in the castle has a computer and there is a professional standard stage to do the plays on and an outdoor one for the hot weather.

I asked Mum if I could go to Daisy's school and she said, 'Apart from the money, it's the principle of the thing.' And she made me stir a huge pail of paint that splashed green blobs all over my white knee socks and there aren't any clean ones in the drawer. Typical Mum.

Just then, Mr Bull came into the gallery and went up to the Piranha's flat to borrow a book. I asked Mum what principles were really and she said, 'What a time to ask.' And she went on crossly slapping this piece of furniture with a painty rag.

A commode, she calls it but it is really an old

fashioned Portaloo and quite an unhygienic idea,
I say.

Principles are –
(a) not eating meat but keeping quiet about it.
(b) not being allowed to go to a school with a
professional standard stage.
I have looked up principle in the dictionary. It
says it is a basic truth.

With love from your friend in England,
Anna Pitts

The Old Butcher's,
Leachfield,
Gloucestershire,
England,
The Planet

January 27th

Dear Clare,
   GOOD NEWS! GOOD NEWS! Just as things
were going from bad to grave, we have got
what Mum calls a commission. Everybody is
laughing and we have had *champagne*! Have you
had it?

   It is like Appeltize to start with, then at the end
of your swallow there is a sort of taste of bad breath
which made me think Mum had got a bottle that
was past its sell-by date but no, that's how
champagne is.

   Mum is going to stencil and stuff a whole house.
Mr Bull pulled some strings and a farmer's wife who

looks more like a model has commissioned mum and she's bought the old fashioned Portaloo too.

Saturday 28th

Clare! A terrible, terrible thing has happened.

I went with Shereen to see about a job collecting eggs and they took me into this place called a Battery House. I could not hear what Shereen was shouting to me over the hen noise. There were hundreds of hens in cages and they smelt and all the hens had bald, pimply patches on them and little, swivelling, sad eyes and no daylight.

I ran out and the owner was there and I said, 'Please let your hens out.'

And he said, 'They are my livelihood, young lady.'

And I said, 'You should not live off cruelty.'

And he said, 'You are an unprepossessing little piece of work if ever I saw one. What's your name?'

And I said, 'Miss Pitts.'

And he said, 'Pitts. Well, I hope your mother doesn't hold the same crackpot ideas as you do. Now, buzz off.'

Oh, Clare. It's his wife that's commissioned Mum to stencil their house. What if he cancels the commission and we go back to being seriously poor and not just poor?

It will be my fault.

Oh, why did I say it?

I wish I was dead.

I have looked up unprepossessing in the dictionary.

With love from your friend in England,
Anna Pitts

The Old Butcher's,
Leachfield,
Gloucestershire,
England,
The Planet

January 31st

Dear Clare,

Quelle terrors the countryside holds!

There is this thing called the W.I. It is a club for women who can make really ace cakes. The Piranha has been smuggling their cakes into her flat and not exactly pretending she made them herself but not saying she didn't and then feeding them to Mr Bull, the reporter. (The Piranha is going to join the W.I. but I don't rate her chances of passing the cake-making test.)

My friend Shereen's mother's sister, Auriol, who cleans the Piranha's flat, let out that these cakes come from the W.I. market which is stalls and stalls and stalls of cakes every Tuesday in Bamford, two miles from here if you take the footpath.

Auriol cleans the Piranha's flat so well, it shows our part of the house up. Yesterday, during tea, a lump of fluff came bowling out from under the kitchen table in the draught from our legs. It was so big, we all thought it was a mouse and had to jump on our chairs but Sis went one step further and jumped on the table and put her foot in my pasta by mistake and skidded off and knocked her face on the floor.

There was blood and spaghetti everywhere. Once we had stuffed her nose with Andrex – no recycled

56

toilet paper! Typical Mum – and washed the kitchen floor, and drenched Sis's jodhpurs from New Gran in Stain Devil for Tar because we hadn't got the one for Blood, Mum said we must all try harder to sweep and stuff but not to worry too much because a bit of dust would make the clients think we were other-worldly artists and that was good for trade.

I think Mum has finally lost her marbles. What other world? I do not look at all Martian even though my roots are coming through as black as ebony.

The girls on the school bus laugh deliberately extra loud when I get on and will not speak. Because of my hair, Sis says. Mum says to ignore them but how do you show someone who is ignoring you that you are ignoring them?

Today, I whistled a medley from the Top Twenty all the way there to show I did not care. When we arrived, the school heating had broken down. The bus turned round and brought us straight back so with the double journey to whistle, by halfway home I got cramp in the lips and had to stop. So they still laughed.

Home was weird on a school day. Like being ill but without feeling rough. There wasn't any real food in our part of the house just something that I think was a swede. I knocked on the Piranha's door for a slice of W.I. cake but there was no answer.

I suddenly realised it was Tuesday and I could walk over and see the fabulous W.I. market for myself and buy a cake too.

Mum was at the back of the shop experimenting with a cauldron of boiling glue so it seemed a good moment to ask her for the five weeks' pocket money she owes me. She said, 'What a time to ask. Can't you think of anything but money, Anna?'

It would be easier to think about other things if Mum paid on the nail each week and I didn't have to worry about where the next penny was coming from. But I didn't say so because Mum is brilliant at economics arguments even though she is poor.

To my surprise, Mr Bull, the reporter, came down from borrowing another book from the Piranha and I asked him why they hadn't answered the door to me just now and he said the bell must be broken.

Just then Mum accidentally sloshed some glue on to the heat and Mr Bull, the reporter, ran to help because it was seething about dangerously and making a stink.

I went into the shop and got a loan of £3 from the till.

No wonder they say never believe a word you read in the papers. Mr Bull, the reporter, must know the Piranha doesn't have a doorbell.

Sis said she wanted to come to Bamford with me. At first I would not let her because I planned to gaze at nature in the chains of mankind and make up the words for my Factory Farming Musical. I have this idea for a chorus of Oven Ready Turkeys and I did not want a meat-eater around to put me off.

Sis said she was a cake eater and you didn't have to kill a cake to eat it and also she was half my sister and also she would tell about the £3 I had nicked from the till if I did not let her come.

Quelle crudité!

There was a cow on the footpath so we took

another route across country. Sis didn't stop moaning about the mud on the trainers New Gran bought her last weekend until we heard this thwack thwacking noise.

Sis said we'd found an Acid Rain house party.

Sis gets muddled.

And then we saw all these men and boys hitting the trees and hedges and bushes with sticks. I guessed we had stumbled on some rustic Freemasons performing their secret rites. Then one of them waved. It was Gerald Tappering who has outgrown his strength so most of what he does looks like waving and I could not be sure what he meant and I told Sis to run.

Next thing, there were bangs and bullets and I fell down and this dog came and stood panting over me and dripped saliva on to my glasses so I could not see at all.

It is a kidnapping, I thought to myself, and I knew in my heart of hearts Mum could never afford the ransom and she would have to live for ever with her remorse for moving away from the safety of 82A, Lucien Road, London, England, The Planet, LIVE ON IT, NOT OFF IT. Typical Mum.

Some people came and stood round us shouting and squelching their feet right by my ear till one of them picked me up and I took my glasses off and I could just see these misty figures all dressed in green like Robin Hood and his men only not so merry. I could hear the whizzing of wings and one of the men shouted more about the line of fire and I realised we had run into a shooting party. Isn't it peculiar how many different sorts of parties there are?

59

The green men all had guns and said the pheasants had got away because of us and we had spoiled their fun. I drew myself up and put on my glasses even though they were dog spitty and said, 'We are townsfolk and know naught of country matters.' Which is William Shakespeare's *Hamlet* or as near as nothing.

I gave them a very Shakespearean look too, which is a half noble, a quarter sad, and a quarter haughty look. If you want to use it at an Australian shooting party, I advise you to practise it in the mirror first because it is not as easy as it sounds.

One green man said, 'Where is this kid from? The funny farm?'

And another one said, 'I know them.'

And oh! Clare! It was the chicken farmer who I had offended. He said, 'They are the Pitts.' And a handsome young one with strawberry cheeks said, 'You can say that again.' And they all laughed.

I could have died.

Another man with a face the colour of plum jam said to us, 'Where do you live? Because I'm jolly well coming to have a word with your father.'

My mind raced.

Sis cried.

Some of the men in green turned out to be ladies in green who hugged Sis and said she was sweet really and the plum man got out his hanky and made her blow her nose and the dog licked her and she didn't scream which was amazingly brave because Sis is as frightened of dogs as I am of cows.

We were put into a Japanese land rover and bounced across the fields to a stately house where a kind cleaning lady all the way from Sri Lanka dried us by the aga and wiped my glasses and gave us Coke and cake to eat so we did not have to buy any at the W.I. market.

Maybe God put the cow on the footpath to save the till money.

Please let me have your opinion on that theory.

9.03 p.m.

A man called Bob has just been. At first I ran into the toilet because he was from the chicken farmer but he gave Mum a dead pheasant and asked if we were all right. Mum gave him a cup of tea and said we were. Bob is a gamekeeper.

Today is the last day they are allowed to shoot so I bet those pheasants that got away were really glad to see Sis and me.

Bob told us Gerald Tappering was being a beater when we saw him. Sis says a beater is an old fashioned hoover but even Gerald Tappering is nothing like a vacuum cleaner.

Not a word about cancelling Mum's commission. Phew! Phew! Mum is all day inventing the stencils. She sings over the washing up.

It is no joke.

With love from your friend in England,
Anna Pitts

P.S. I have looked up beater in the dictionary. It is a living scarecrow which is quite a good fit for Gerald Tappering. I am going to have a serious talk with him about it even though he has outgrown his strength. A.P.

The Old Butcher's,
Leachfield,
Gloucestershire,
England,
The Planet
(But really I am in Barryard bus shelter)

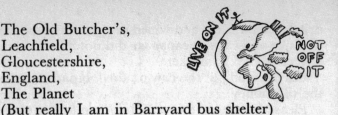

February 5th

Dear Clare,

Bob, the gamekeeper, has been to see how Sis and me are three times in a week and each time he brings Mum something dead to cook which is really disgusting but Mum says not to look a gift horse in the mouth. When I said we didn't eat horses, she said, 'Oh shut up, Anna.' Which is a bit strange when you think how keen she is on my principles.

Today, the Piranha made us go to church in Bamford.

I am not wild about church since God took that fiver from my Christmas present money but the Piranha wouldn't budge and said I must go.

When Sis came downstairs in her latest gear from New Gran, the Piranha said, 'I am not taking you looking like lolita.' Sis did not know what a lolita is so she couldn't decide whether to cry or not.

New Gran, who is down for the weekend, comme toujours, went all angry and red. Mum raced her and the Piranha off into the kitchen so Sis and me wouldn't hear the row. But we did.

Then out bounced New Gran and swept Sis away in her Vauxhall so I guess a lolita is not good news.

Mum said she'd got a headache from the strain. That left just the Piranha and me in the church party.

On the way, in the Rover, I asked the Piranha if she had some great sorrow that we were going to church about.

She said, 'I am not a foul weather Christian, Anna. Going to church is good for trade.'

Just then, she nearly killed a goose that was crossing the road so I did not ask her what she meant but left her to concentrate.

It is funny that lumps of fluff and church are both good for trade. They are not at all alike.

I looked up lolita in the dictionary during the kitchen row but it was not there. Please look in your dictionary and let me know. Sis is convinced it is an Italian iced lolly but I think it might be rude.

Church was really boring. The hymns were too high and there wasn't any bopping. During the sermon, a terrible, terrible thought came to me.

The priest was telling this horror story from the Bible about killing a fatted calf and I remembered the stockman who is making his living from cruelty and will pulverise his son.

And then I thought of the chicken farmer who is making his living from cruelty.

And then I thought of Mum who is making her living from the chicken farmer.

And then I realised that when Mum buys my pasta, she will be buying it with cruelty money, even though it is gained artistically.

I could not help it but the tears came out of my

eyes. The Piranha was furious. At first, she tried pushing a tissue behind my glasses but it soaked through and so she made me go out.

Wet wads of tissue fell off my face on to the floor all the way up the aisle. Everyone stared.

I could have died.

God certainly paid me back for bringing up that fiver.

When I got out, someone called my name. At first I thought it was God having another go but it was my new friend, Shereen, with lots of other girls and a boy from Seniors.

Shereen said, 'This is Andrew, Anna.'

And he said, 'Hello, Anna.'

And I said, 'Hello.'

Andrew has got dark brown hair and quizzical eyes that match it and lightly tanned skin and when he smiles, it is just like George Michael.

'Come and help,' he said. 'We are going to clean up the bus shelter.'

We all had brushes and white emulsion and we painted out every single rude word people had written on the shelter.

I knew all of them except one but there was no sign of a lolita. Shereen said there wasn't on her half either so I guess it is foreign rude.

When we'd finished, Andrew collected our brushes and said we girls were a great team and went into the pub and my heart went with him. So did some of the girls.

The Piranha's Rover was still parked in the square so I bought a Mars bar and a Biro and this letter paper from the newsagents so I could tell you about Andrew while I waited for her.

When I said to the man in the shop, 'This paper is not recycled,' he said, 'I should blinking well hope not.' Then he added really spitefully, 'But the Mars bar is.'

I put the lot on Mum's paper bill and left the shop sadly.

Perhaps people here don't worry about the ecology like Londoners do which is strange because the ecology shows more in the country. Do Australians in the Bush seem more carefree on the subject than Sydney folk?

Still no Piranha so I checked the church. It was empty except for Gerald Tappering who has out-grown his strength. He was wavering about in a long red dress trying to snuff out the candles. The dress is because he is a church server. That is the uniform.

Isn't it strange the way all the priests and archbishops etc. dress up in girls' clothes when they are so dead against lady vicars?

'Hello, Gerald Tappering,' I called. And he jumped so he knocked the candle out of its stick and it burnt a black mark on the altar's table cloth.

He was really scared about it so we scrubbed at it with water from a nearby vase of flowers. We didn't have any tissues but while we were looking, I found the £3 I had forgotten to return to the till. In the end we used the hem of his red costume. The burn came out and the pink patch where the dye ran hardly showed.

While we were doing that, I had a serious talk with him about how his vow to be a vegetarian did not tie in with his job as a beater who scares the pheasants so they fly about getting shot down.

He asked me to come to the pictures with him

in town but I told him to keep to the point.

He said he earned money being a beater and his mum needed it because his dad had been put on half time. So we were back to the cruelty money. I was depressed.

He asked me to go to the pictures with him again. I said no and went out. He called after me that he really enjoyed being a beater. Being a beater was great. I replied I would sooner go to the pictures with a tapeworm than with him.

Outside, the Piranha's Rover had gone so I went to the pub to find my friend Shereen.

Have you ever had a drink called Babycham? It is much nicer than champagne they say and cheaper too. Andrew and all of us sat in the family room. Then I put the £3 from the till towards a round of St Clements.

And Andrew said, 'Cheers, Anna.' And then he said, 'I really like your hair style.'

And then he smiled at me.

And it was the best day of my life.

With love from your friend in England,
Anna Pitts

P.S. The Piranha still hasn't shown up so I'll walk home – on air. A.P.

The Old Butcher's,
Leachfield,
Gloucestershire,
England,
The Planet

February 8th

Dear Clare,

I have got a Saturday morning job and am saving
up to come and live with you in Australia. It is clear
to me my family will not miss me at all.

As I was walking home after the St Clements, I
met Mr Bull, the reporter, hurrying along the path.
He said, 'My God! You are here.' And he looked
strangely sorry. He was all puffed and holding one
hand on to where your heart is only it's on the
inside, of course.

'Your grandmother burst in on your mother and
me,' he said, 'and lost her rag totally.' I asked him
why but he did not answer, just panted out, 'She
says you have been abducted and now all the police
are looking for you.'

I told him I was in the pub and he said one of
the bus shelter words in a low voice and ran on to
try and find the Piranha who, he said, was driving
slowly up and down the lanes looking for my body.

I think Mr Bull will know what a lolita is.

When I reached the Old Butcher's, Bob the
gamekeeper was there, with a dead drake,
comforting Mum who was on the phone to the
police. When she saw me, she dropped the phone
and hugged me so hard she squashed my nose
nearly out through my ears.

'Are you all right? Are you all right?' she asked a lot of times but eventually, I smiled soothingly and said I'd been in the pub all the time. And Mum went berserk.

Isn't it funny the way they do that? One minute they're crying and weeping over your death and as soon as they know you're ok they shout at you and call you selfish and threaten to kill you so you would have been better off dead anyway.

I shall earn £4 every Saturday 9 a.m.–1 p.m. at my job with some organic market gardeners called Will and Belinda who knit all their own clothes in unusual colours.

A single to Australia is £643. I will be sixteen and a half years old by the time I have saved that but I'm counting on the Piranha to top it up once I've put down a bit to show willing. I know she will cough up eagerly as she is the angriest with me about church and the pub and being dead in the lanes because it's caused a rift between her and Mr Bull for some reason and she can no longer give him W.I. cake.

Mum is the second angriest with me as it has caused a rift between her and the Piranha and the Piranha has ordered a builder to make her a separate front door so there are no more ugly scenes she says, whatever that means. And now there is even more dust in our house than usual from the big hole in the wall the builder made before he went away to work on another urgent job.

Sis told me New Gran was driving her back from a really amazing Sunday dinner in a pub where they had sticky toffee pudding and cream for afters, when they met Mr Bull rushing about in the road. He was looking for the Piranha who was in her Rover searching for my body so they drove him round to help find her.

He told New Gran he was pleased I was safe but a bit sad too because it meant he had lost 'one hell of a scoop.' Sis did no know what a scoop is – well, she thought it was a portion of ice cream – but I have looked it up in the dictionary and I must say I am really, really hurt that Mum goes on speaking to Mr Bull and inviting him to supper.

I have warned Sis not to tell that she was in a pub or she will land in dead trouble too.

When they met up with the Piranha, Mr Bull opened the door to get into the Rover but, Sis says, the Piranha shouted, 'Keep away from me you antique Don—.' Sis can't remember what surname she shouted, it was like, Who Iron, she says, but as Mr Bull's name is Phillip and not Donald it is something of a mystery anyway.

Sis said New Gran laughed till her mascara ran and the Piranha tore off so fast she knocked Mr Bull the reporter off balance and he fell over into the hedge.

Mr Bull is third angriest with me –

(a) because his rift with the Piranha means no more cake.

(b) because I'm not dead so he can't have his scoop and be the first reporter to write a sorrowful article in praise of me and

(c) because he twisted his ankle climbing out of the hedge.

The Headmaster is the fourth angriest with me because the police telephoned the school on Monday and the Head called all the girls up to his office who had painted the bus shelter with Andrew.

The Head is a ferocious man. There is a rumour he has only given up corporal punishment on paper.

Of us all, only Shereen and me were at school that day so we got a row that should have been spread more thinly over ten other girls.

It turns out that Andrew was supposed to paint the bus shelter by himself because he is doing something called community service.

When I suggested community service sounded like a good cause and many hands make light work the Head said he always punished impertinence very heavily.

To change the subject, and take his mind off corporal punishment, I asked him if he knew what a lolita was. It was risky because of it maybe being rude. It worked like magic though.

He immediately telephoned the Senior Mistress to come and join us in his office. Then he had a think and then he telephoned the Nurse to come up as well and me and the Senior Mistress and Nurse all went to the medical room. Nurse asked me if I had anything I wanted to tell her.

I really, really racked my brains to think of something because I like the School Nurse and I did not want to disappoint her but in the end, I had to say no.

Then, to my surprise, in flew Mum. She was all wrapped in shawls and her hair tied in a scarf but not properly tied. Typical Mum. And long red strands were hanging out.

I pray and pray Mum will learn to dress like a real person but so far, no luck.

Next thing, she hugged me and shouted, 'Are you all right?' Over and over. My mum is so embarrassing. It was obvious I was all right. 'Tell me all about it,' she said.

The penny dropped. Corporal punishment is against Mum's beliefs and Mum thought the Headmaster had hit me. Mum can't half get hold of the wrong end of the stick sometimes.

I did not want to show her up in front of the senior mistress, so I said significantly, 'He never touched me.' And she cast her eyes to the medical room ceiling and gave this sigh of relief that was really over the top and hugged me lots more and said she'd take me home. The Senior Mistress said she wanted a word with Mum so I went to wait in Mum's car.

The Senior Mistress escorted Mum out. No one saw Mum's gear. Phew! Phew! They were all still in class. Mum smiled and I smiled and we waved goodbye and after a couple of goes at it, we drove off.

And quite out of the blue, Mum turned into a raving scorpion.

How dare I give them all such a scare at school?

How could I give her such a fright?

What had got into me these days?

What had got into *me*!

Then she said in her special bringing up children voice, how I knew perfectly well not to report private, family conversations because talking about lolita caused people – wait for it – to get hold of the wrong end of the stick.

To calm her down, I asked her what Don Who Iron is. After she had re-entered the earth's atmosphere, she said it was Juan not Iron and didn't I talk about anything but sex these days. As you know, my mum harps on sex rather a lot so I did not encourage her to go on.

Just then it started to pour with rain and by the time we'd got the umbrellas up and fixed so Mum could still see to drive but we were catching the leaks too, she'd dropped lolita and Juan and was on about skinning Bob the gamekeeper's latest gift which is an eel.

I am hitting the delete on lolita too. It's bad news. If you go on researching it, here is a clue. As it causes multi mega freak out at school and in the home it's probably drugs.

I think Mum has nearly moved to the top of the Who Is Angriest With Me League.

9:30 p.m.

A vicar came to see Mum about the altar's cloth and the pink burn. Mum parted with a lot of cash to help keep the roof on the church.

Mum has definitely overtaken the Piranha in the W.I.A.W.M. League. Just when I need to ask her a favour too about borrowing her bike on Wednesday nights which is a v.v. spesh night.

Tomorrow, I will break the news to her that I'm moving in with you and Mr and Mrs Hannock and offer her the unique opportunity to top up my fare to Australia. That will cheer her up.

Do they have churches in Australia?

Sorry it's Friday February 10th now

I forgot to ask Mum about Australia or her bike because we were making pancakes. Sis and me did ok but Mum dropped one. Unfortunately it was too floor fluffy to eat.

Sis has solved the Lolita mystery. Her friend Daisy asked around the castle school. It is child pornography for people who read the heavy newspapers. Sis is v. pleased at being called one and got New Gran to buy her the *Times* but she has gone back to *My Little Pony* now.

All the girls who were with me and Andrew in the pub came back to school on Tuesday with my hair style. It is called the Tiger Tint and costs £8.50 at Monday half-price rate at Hair Razors in Bamford.

With love from your friend in England (but not for long),

Anna Pitts

P.S. We girls from the school bus are going to hold a Beauty Tips Evening. I am planning a little talk on Blusher Technique. A.P.

P.P.S. I have looked up Don Juan in the dictionary. He is not there. A.P.

P.P.P.S. He is in Mum s Encyclopaedia. It is a Spanish flirt. Mr Bull the reporter does not look the least Spanish. A.P.

P.P.P.P.S. Never skin an eel. A.P.

The Old Butcher's,
Leachfield,
Gloucestershire,
England,
The Planet

Sunday February 12th

Dear Clare,
    I've done my first Saturday morning at my job.
It is rather cold being an organic gardener. Mum
says you have to be dedicated.
    My fingers felt strange and when I scraped the
mud off for a look, they were dead white like frozen
chips before they are cooked but I did not say
anything in case Will and Belinda thought I was
too weak for the job.
    They have a baby called Dan who rambles
round the garden in little knitted clothes and does
not feel the cold a scrap except his nose runs. It
runs into his mouth. Apart from that, he is quite
fun.
    At one o'clock, they gave me £4.
    Australia here I come!

2:30 p.m.
    I am down to £1.
    At Sunday dinner, I was just going to broach the
subject of Mum's bike and Wednesday nights when
Mum said the shop's accounts were £3 out so I
explained I'd borrowed it.
    Quelle row!
    Mum said it was stealing and New Gran who is
down for the weekend, comme toujours, said I had

been mixing with criminal elements. And Mr Bull, the reporter, who is always at Sunday lunch now as well as supper, said, 'Steady on.' Sis cried.

'What criminal elements?' asked Mum. And New Gran said, 'That Andrew character she is sweet on. He's a bad lot and a bad influence.'

I picked up my spaghetti from my plate and draped it over her head.

I am in my room now and in love with Andrew.

I have paid back the £3.

New Gran has gone home to London.

No matter how they smear his character, the smile Andrew gave me, they can never take away. Never, never.

I could really do with that spaghetti now.

Don't worry if you haven't got a spare room in Australia. I shall be travelling light.

Why is it stealing to take £3 from the till but not stealing not to pay up five weeks' pocket money?

With love from your friend in England,
Anna Pitts

P.S. Don't tell your mum and dad about me coming to live with them. I want it to be a surprise. A.P.

P.P.S. If the Piranha is right about Australia being full of escaped convicts, with me being a thief, I shall blend in nicely. A.P.

The Old Butcher's,
Leachfield,
Gloucestershire,
England

SAVE OUR PLANET FROM ITS
PLIGHT

February 15th

Dear Prime Minister,

Very soon, I shall be living in Australia because my family have cast me out but before I go, I want you to think about barges.

Yesterday, a juggernaut came by and knocked a huge hole in my grandmother's flat which is a shame because the builders have only just finished knocking a hole in it to make her a front door. But enough of personal tragedies.

If what was in the juggernaut had been in a barge sailing along one of Britain's many delightful water-ways, the juggernaut would not have been driving down our road or been in collision with our house.

The dirty fuel would not have been polluting our countryside and sending the children mad and tossing a blanket of CO_2 into the atmosphere so that our world will become unbearably hot.

The canals are waiting in all their sleepy charm. All it needs is a law from you.

The barges can be built by the unemployed so that's one worry off your shoulders. The horses to pull the barges will be happy to breed and you can make good use of their dung.

I hope you will act on this advice.

Yours sincerely,

Anna Pitts

Aged 13

The Old Butcher's,
Leachfield,
Gloucestershire,
England,
The Planet

February 16th

Dear Clare,
  Would you believe it? Mum got three Valentines which is quite freakish in one so old. Sis got seven. I did not send any this year.
  The Piranha has gone to stay with one of her ex-husband's widows because her flat has been knocked over by a lorry and the builders are in. The Old Butcher's is shaped

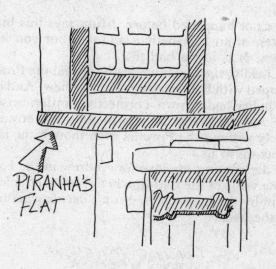

PIRANHA'S
FLAT

like this (or was)

So it is plain for all to see that the top is too big for the bottom and a miracle that aerial accidents of this type

have not happened before. Mum says this bit* is a gem of an Elizabethan addition but you know Mum. It is just a bad fit.

Luckily, there was no death toll and the Piranha escaped with light grazing. Phew! Phew! And once the police had thrown a protective cordon between her and the driver he was ok too. It is strangely lonely without the Piranha even though she is not speaking to us.

I am carving my love for Andrew in the harsh, stone walls of the Old Butcher's, or what is left of them by the juggernaut. I can't decide whether to do the usual

or or even

so I have had to stop at the first A also I have broken Mum's Stanley knife. Please let me have your opinion on the above.

I wait in the school corridor every free minute I have to see Andrew go by. I've glimpsed him four times but so far our eyes have not met. I think this is because so many girls are standing around in the way.

Shereen, my new friend, says they are all waiting to see Andrew go by too but I will not be stung into a frenzy of jealousy.

Last night at supper, Mum remarked to Mr Bull, the reporter, that she always put her children first.

Sis cried.

In the end, we decided it was with pleasure.

I went into the toilet for a hollow laugh.

9:30 p.m.

Bob, the gamekeeper, came to see us to ask us how we enjoyed his eel. Mum gave me one of her frowns so I did not tell him.

While she was making my cocoa, Mum remarked to Bob that she always put her children first.

Sis would have cried but she was in bed.

Bob gave me a Yorkie Bar. I dissolved it in my cocoa.

They said I was disgusting.

So all in all, it was a happy evening.

Tomorrow, I will have a serious talk with Mum about topping up my fare to Australia and lending me her bike on Wednesday nights which is a mega urgent matter.

With love from your friend in England,
Anna Pitts

P.S. I cannot work out who Mum's third Valentine card was from. A.P.

The Old Butcher's,
Leachfield,
Gloucestershire,
England,
The Planet

February 21st

Dear Clare,

Now hear this! Now hear this! Anna Pitts is going to be a bridesmaid. Ra ra ra. My first time.

Shereen, my new friend's mother's sister, Auriol, who cleans for the Piranha (except she's had to stop because the Piranha's flat is being rebuilt) is getting married and she's asked me and Shereen to be bridesmaids.

Our dresses will be mostly apricot but with coffee trimmings. Sis says they are naf colours, she is moody though because she didn't go shopping last weekend.

Imagine – a whole weekend without New Gran

(because of the Pasta and Head incident). It was almost spooky.

The wedding is in April. I am practising the walk every day in Mum's dressing gown to get used to the length.

When Mum asked Auriol if she was going to wear white, she said definitely off white, and they both laughed.

Quelle crudité!

I must finish now and assemble my blusher collection. It is us bus girls' Beauty Tip Session this afternoon at Shereen's. She's doing the records and mirrors and we bring our own make-up kit, Diet Coke and Yorkie Bars.

Do you get half term in Australia?

With love from your friend in England,
Anna Pitts

P.S. I got a Valentine in the post this morning. One week late. It is Gerald Tappering's writing. A.P.

P.P.S. When you write to me after summer camp, please check you put the right amount of stamps on. A.P.

P.P.S. £5 saved now so I will be coming to live with you immediately after Auriol's wedding in April. It will be your Autumn then so I will not feel the heat so badly. Should I have one of those hats with corks hanging from the brim? If so, please buy me one as I do not want to be the odd one out. I will pay you back when I get there. A.P.

The Old Butcher's,
Leachfield,
Gloucestershire,
England,

The Planet

February 25th

Dear Clare,
    There is a slight complication about my trip to
Australia. I own a hen called Ethel.
    Please let me know at once if it
is all right to bring her with me.
She only needs a garden and a
shed and I'm sure she will start
laying lots of eggs soon.
    I have been studying the map
of Australia, my home to be.
Why are all the towns
round the edge? Is there
something wrong with the middle?
    The Beauty Tips afternoon was a
wash-out. A girl called Carol brought this magazine
all about the cruel tests the make-up people do on
rabbits and other little animals. There were pictures
of them doing it too and I had to take my glasses
off.
    Then Shereen went to her kitchen and fetched
a dustbin liner and one by one, we threw our make-
up kits into it. Shereen had to use an overspill bag
because she had got so much.
    Then we wrote out a huge notice to pin on the
school board when we go back next week to warn

all the other girls in the school that they are spreading cruelty to animals on their faces.

Then we all tissued off our make-up for the very last time and ate our Yorkie Bars.

Five minutes later

I have just been down to the garden to see if Ethel has laid an egg yet but so far, no luck.

Walking back from Shereen's without my blusher on I felt rather underdressed. Also my cheeks grew cold from exposure. I kept my head sunk forward so as not to shock a passing pedestrian. I didn't meet anyone though. Phew! Phew!

A motor bike that drove by hooted out that Colonel Bogey tune most rudely but I pretended not to care for the sake of the little rats etc.

Ten minutes later

Do you suppose if Ethel sat down and rested she might lay an egg? She spends all day scratching the garden with her claws. At first I thought she was looking for something she'd lost but now I think more likely it is her hobby. Bob, the gamekeeper, gave her to Sis and me.

Yesterday, when Mr Bull, the reporter, was introduced to Ethel, he jingled the money in his pockets and then he said, 'Well, well. So that's his game.'

I explained to Mr Bull that Ethel is a hen and not a game bird but he only looked at me in rather a mad fashion. Sometimes I think Mr Bull is not quite all there.

Bob picked Ethel out for Sis and me because she was the same colour as Mum's hair. Mum smiled when he said it but then she has a peculiar sense of humour.

Sis told me afterwards she wanted a whole pet and not half a hen, whatever colour it was, and I could have all of Ethel to myself.

But I made her put it in writing.

Sis is still v. moody. She seems to have gone on strike as a person except to make a long, reverse charge call to New Gran. New Gran hasn't been back since the Pasta and Head incident so now, with the Piranha away, there is a shortage of grandmothers as well as dads in our family.

One hour later

I have decided to sacrifice some of my Australian fare and buy Sis a hamster. Then she will cheer up and forget all about New Gran.

And so can we.

7 p.m.

Bob, the gamekeeper, has just gone.

Ethel does not understand about going to bed in her shed and dashes round the garden in a scatty way when we try to catch her.

Mum had to keep ringing Bob to come over and help us so now he drops in every twilight specially to lend me a hand which is really nice of him. And then Mum gives him a glass of wine and we make conversation.

This evening, we roasted chestnuts too. Mum seemed to forget all about the fact that I don't rate roasted chestnuts. So rather impolitely, I slipped gradually out of the room. Bob didn't notice. Phew! Phew!

I'm not so sure about Mum.

Mr Bull, the reporter, came for supper. He brought Sis a hamster. Which saved me the bother.

He told me my new slogan – PROTECT AND SURVIVE – was invented by Mrs Thatcher's government so great minds think alike.

Mr Bull's limp from where the Piranha knocked him over is much better. He said the doctor had sent him twice a week for physiotherapy and told him categorically to cut out the booze. He was v. cheerful about that and laughed so loudly, Sis and me could not hear the television.

When we sat down to supper, he said, 'Hello, where's all our wine got to?' Which makes him pretty forgetful for a reporter or even just a regular person.

I explained about Ethel my hen, and Bob's glass of wine.

Mr Bull went out to his car to fetch another bottle but I think something urgent must have arisen in his reporting work because he didn't come back. Sis and Mum shared his supper between them.

We tried to choose a name for Sis's hamster. Mum wanted Harry the Hamster but Sis said that Harry was too royal. I suggested Hercules and Sis said no, she had decided on Willie. So I came up to bed and left it to Mum to explain. After all, Mum is Sis's mother.

They are still mumbling away down there. But then Sis is very slow for her age.

Another weekend without New Gran!

85

With love from your friend in England,
Anna Pitts

P.S. Sis has just jétèd in to tell me her final decision on the hamster's name. He is called John. As you know, that is the name of the art student, my dad. A.P.

P.P.S. Can sisters apply for legal separation in Australia? A.P.

P.P.P.S. Last night, I dreamed it was Wednesday night and Mum's bike had no wheels! A.P.

The Old Butcher's,
Leachfield,
Gloucestershire,
England,
The Planet

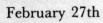

February 27th

Dear Clare,
   Oh, no. Oh, no. Oh, no. A really, really awful thing has happened.
   Everyone was in school. I was late because I'd been pinning our notice about make-up and cruelty to animals on the board. As I was hurrying down the corridor to class, who should be in the distance walking towards me?
   ANDREW!!
   My heart leapt. To be truthful, it felt more like my stomach made a bid for freedom. My legs went to pasta (cooked).
   He came nearer and nearer. Our first moment

alone together. My mind whirled to think up something tempting to say. He was a metre away.

I said, 'Hello.'

He smiled. I smiled. He said, 'Hi, Anthea,' and walked on past me.

Anthea!

Why, oh why didn't I stop him and say I'm Anna not Anthea?

Suddenly, he turned back and said, 'By the way, Anthea.' And oh, no. Oh, no. Oh, no. Instead of saying it then either, I answered, 'Yes, Andrew?' It came out in a sort of croaky whisper.

I could have died.

He smiled.

I willed Nurse to come down the corridor with a life support machine.

'Sorry about your spot of bother with the Head,' he said.

Nurse hadn't shown up so I said, 'That's all right,' in another croaky whisper.

I had this faint worry he might think I was turning into a frog. Then I thought turning into a frog would be better than the current situation and I could live out the rest of my days in a distant ditch – a broken-hearted, endangered species. But no such luck. I stayed a girl.

'I tried to have a word with you when I passed you on the bike,' he said, 'but you ignored me.'

Oh, Clare. It was him who hooted Colonel Bogey.

I cleared my throat. 'I didn't hear you hoot.' My voice boomed down the corridor like we were in an echo chamber. I could have died.

He smiled.

You don't have to be Sherlock Holmes to work out that if I didn't hear him hoot, how did I know he'd hooted.

I was so hot I must have run a temperature.

'Cheers, Anthea,' he said. And walked away.

What am I going to do??? Why did I miss that little minute when I could have said I was Anna? Twice! I feel such a fool. He will think I am a fool if he finds out my true name. Do you think I should write to him? Ring?

Please let me have your opinion on this immediately.

I will ask Mum if I can change to another school. I can't face him.

Ever.

After he'd gone, I ran into the toilets. My face was like it had been dusted all over in blusher. I held it in a wash hand basin full of cold water till it went its usual colour. It took half an hour.

Once, I nearly drowned because I breathed in by mistake. It gave me a sore throat and nose ache for the rest of the day.

6:02 p.m.

I have telephoned the vicar to ask him to christen me Anthea. I told him I wanted a simple, private ceremony, just him and me. He said he would think about it.

With love from your friend in England,
Anna Pitts

The Old Butcher's,
Leachfield,
Gloucestershire,
England,
The Planet

March 2nd

Dear Clare,

Would you believe? New Gran sent Sis a pony this morning. It is shaggy and small and it has bitten Mr Bull on the bottom.

At first, Mum did not agree with the man who delivered it that the pony was for us and she tried to send it back but he insisted it was definitely ours.

Then she rang up New Gran but she was out making a film for the television. Then the man put the pony in our garden and drove off and Mum hit the ceiling.

She was really angry because it had no equipment and no operator's manual with it and she said it would have to go back.

Sis cried.

We missed school.

Then Mr Bull turned up. We haven't seen him since he went to get a bottle of wine and never came back. He had a box of plonk, he called it, for Bob, the gamekeeper, so Bob wouldn't drink his claret, he said.

Mum was really pleased to see him because Mr Bull said he knew all about horses from reporting gymkhanas, which are a sort of sports day for ponies, and he patted the pony, who is called, Bunjie and shouted, 'Hi ho, Silver,' and it was then it bit his bottom.

Next thing, it went running round the garden and Ethel, my hen, went running round too just in front of it and Mr Bull, the reporter, was running round on the spot holding his bitten bottom. And Mum screeched unspeakables about New Gran, and I screamed and ran after Ethel to rescue her from Bunjie's plunging hooves and Mr Bull roared, 'Ow! Ow! Ow!'

Sis laughed.

Then Ethel flew with a hoppy clatter up into the apple tree so Bunjie changed course and ran after poor Mr Bull to bite him some more and Mr Bull called for help in sobbing gasps as he sped round the flower beds with Bunjie at his heels.

Just then, the Piranha came home and spoke in a voice of thunder, 'Whoa!' And Bunjie stood stock still at once and Mum got the car, shut the shop, and went to town to go to the hospital with Mr Bull and the library for a book on horses.

The Piranha went away again. She only called in to pick up a cashmere wrap and tear a strip off her builders.

Sis rang her friend Daisy's mother and she came over with a Land Rover full of pony nuts (which aren't nuts at all) and hay and stuff and a lot of leather straps for Bunjie to wear. I was forced to slave away with Sis cleaning out Ethel's bedroom shed for him which, according to Daisy's mum, was originally a loose box.

Sis was really excited and they led Bunjie into his sparkling stable and Daisy's mum said, 'You'll be hunting him, of course?'

And Sis replied, 'Of course.'

But Daisy's mum has not watched Sis try to play hunt the thimble. If she had, she might not have brought the subject up.

2 p.m.

Mum isn't back yet. Sis has taken my missed school packed lunch up the garden for a picnic with Bunjie in his stable. She has given me John the hamster as payment. I have accepted him on condition I can change his name to Gains-borough.

3:45 p.m.

I was starving.

There wasn't much food in the kitchen and anyway it was all stuff for meat-eaters. Eventually, I found a litre of Coca Cola but that wasn't totally filling. Then I came across last night's left over pasta and fried it up.

I had not realised pasta is so inflammable but I easily put out the flames with the last of the Coke which caused a bit of smoke.

One of the Piranha's builders came down to see what the smell was and if they ought to call the fire brigade. He gave me a Walls meat pie.

I did not like to hurt his feelings so I said to myself I would take a bite and then throw it in the waste bin when he had gone back to work which he quickly did because the Piranha has told them she is going to take them all to court for not rebuilding her flat fast enough.

Mum still isn't back.

4:45 p.m.

I took a step ladder into the garden to fetch Ethel down from the apple tree. She flapped so hard at me that I toppled off the steps. At first, I thought I was dead but after I'd lain there a while I decided I had only broken my skeleton in many places.

The relief of knowing I could spend a year or so in a plaster cast, in a remote hospital, very far away from Andrew, was fantastic.

Just then, Sis came by and asked what I was doing lying on my back under the apple tree. I instructed her calmly, so as not to scare her, to call an ambulance because I had multiple injuries and would have to be invalided out of school.

Sis said she had seen me through the kitchen window stuffing a whole meat pie and I was a phoney vegetarian.

I sprang up to kill her and she said I was a phoney invalid too.

I think I preferred Sis when she was on strike as a person.

Mum still isn't back yet.

Sorry, it's March 3rd now, 9:30 p.m.

Bunjie would not share the shed with Ethel. She is sleeping in the attic next to mine till Bob brings her a pheasant coop.

When Bob and me first put Ethel in with him, Bunjie tried to kick her but she dodged and so he got me instead. Mum drove back to the hospital again for me to have an X-ray.

I have a bruise shaped like this and these truly, cross my heart, are the measurements. It is yellow, green and blue. New Gran is revenged for the Pasta and Head incident.

15 cm

20 cm

On the way home, at midnight, there was a good opportunity to have a serious yet cosy talk with Mum. I asked her to change my school.

She said no.

I told her I was going to Australia. She asked what was the point then of changing school if I was changing countries and agreed I could borrow her bike on Wednesdays once she had fixed the front brake.

Then she asked me what this christening was that the vicar was on about. I said it was a private matter and in future I wanted to be called Anthea.

She said she would try but old habits die hard.
That vicar is a creep.
With love from your friend in England,
Anna Pitts

To:-
HM The Queen,
Buckingham Palace,
London,
England,
The Planet

March 4th

Your Majesty,
I know you are never without a dog and have a
wonderful way with animals because my
grandmother told me. Now here is a golden
opportunity to help them too.
Did you know you can buy make-up that has not
used experiments on animals to make it? I didn't.
The things that go on in your kingdom must
sometimes take even you by surprise.
What's more, some of this make-up comes
in delicious flavours like raspberry and black-
currant etc. which means one can have a quiet
eat if one runs into a boring moment. So HURRY,
HURRY and Appoint a Supplier while stocks
last.
Please pass this letter on to your daughter and
daughters-in-law and your mother and sister.
Ordinarily I would send them their own letter but

I don't want to waste the money on stamps as I am saving all my wages to leave England forever.

Your servant,
Anna Pitts
Aged 13

P.S. Don't worry, I shall still be your subject as Australia is my destination. A.P.

The Old Butcher's,
Leachfield,
Gloucestershire,
England,
The Planet

Monday March 6th

Dear Clare,

I am not speaking to Shereen. Ever again. One day/week/year, I will tell you why. When I can bear the pain.

Sorry it's Saturday 11th now

Bob, the gamekeeper, has given me a coop for Ethel. Mum stencilled her name over the door. I expect Ethel to lay an egg any day now.

Bob showed us how to muck out Bunjie's stable.

Bunjie bit my head.

Luckily, he only got my hair and tore a small lump out. I still do not have enough to spare for that so I went to borrow one of the Piranha's builder's safety helmets but they were just about leaving. They have finished her flat amazingly quickly. I had to put on one of mum's saucepans instead which turned out to be simpler than getting it off.

Eventually, Mum, Bob and the builders did it with soap and the bricky's mallet.

If ever you find yourself caught with a saucepan stuck on your head in Australia I do not advise you to allow them to use that method because they forget your neck is not a corkscrew and waste too much valuable time laughing.

Sis and Mum are looking for a paddock for Bunjie. I favour a prairie. In Outer Mongolia.

I wheel a barrow of Bunjie's manure with me to work at Will and Belinda's organic garden.

It steams.

It is a whole mile.

I pray and pray no one will see and smell me on the way but Mum says it is a chance to put my principles into practice and besides, there is nowhere else to dump the stuff. I have found a way though of fixing my anorak collar right up to my eyes, like this so I can travel incognito and keep out the stink.

Today I was pushing my barrow when I met Shereen on her bike.

She said, 'Hello, Anna. What a pong!'

I sank inside my anorak in a dignified fashion and would not speak.

96

Mr Bull, the reporter took us to a theme park. He said it was to get us off Mum's hands so she could complete her designs for the chicken farmer's wife's house.

We could not set out until the afternoon because of my job at the organic garden and Sis's riding lesson and dance class.

On the way, we had to stop because suddenly the lane was full of dogs and it was the hunt. I have never seen one before.

You can't now because you are no longer a Pommie but they look exactly like they do on Christmas cards only on fast forward and without the snow.

Two huntsmen on huge, beautiful horses held up the traffic. Mr Bull said the men were wearing hunting pink but really it was more the colour the Red Coats wear at Butlin's holiday camp only the jacket is more tightly waisted.

The hounds went straight through the hedge and over a field and a lot of riders in elegant clothes went racing after them.

Mr Bull shouted 'Tallyho,' over the noise, and took a photograph for his paper and knew one of the men on the huge horses. Sis was v. impressed.

The man said they had killed a fox that day and Mr Bull said, 'Jolly good.' And Sis and me said, 'Triff.' And we drove on.

But what if the fox's children are waiting for her to come home?

Mr Bull's car makes me feel sick.

When we got to the theme park, it was nearly closing time. The rides were v. low on terror. Mr

Bull screamed non-stop but Sis and me reckoned they couldn't touch Alton Towers.

On the way home, I was sick.

Later, Sis was too.

Then I was again.

Shereen has just phoned. I told Sis to say I was at the disco.

When we got back from the theme park, Mr Bull called out, 'Here's your little brood,' and opened the door. Mum and Bob, the gamekeeper, were sitting having a drink of Mr Bull's wine in a box.

Mr Bull gabbled something in a whisper and before Sis and me had time to thank him because, to be fair, I think he had meant it to be fun, he said loudly that he would be off and whizzed outside and there was the Piranha standing by a pile of luggage undoing the many locks on her new front door.

The Piranha smiled really nicely at Mr Bull so obviously their rift is over. Phew! Phew!

'Dear lady,' said Mr Bull, 'welcome home. Let me please,' and tried to yank a bag off the top of the pyramid of her cases.

'Don't bother, Phil,' she said to Mr Bull, 'James will see to it. And James came from putting his Daimler away and picked up four big cases, two in each hand, and took them into the Piranha's flat. And Mr Bull went away.

James is a little bit like Simon, the lodger we had. Did I ever mention him to you? But James is old. He is twenty-seven.

He is the chauffeur of the widow of one of the Piranha's ex-husbands and drove the Piranha home.

He is staying over the weekend with the Piranha

to help her with her new carpet. They are going to lay it together.

Shereen has telephoned again. She told Sis I am not at the disco because she is at it and I'm not there. She wants to explain and it isn't her fault. Huh! Oh the pain!

Tomorrow, Sis and Bunjie go hunting for the first time. New Gran has sent Sis all the riding gear you need to hunt from Bond Street. Also a special hat so she cannot damage her brain when she falls on her head. Which is shutting the stable door if you ask me.

I must stop now and finish *Arable Agony*, my factory farming musical. At first I ran into problems with my tunes because Butch Hills, whose face is like a plate of muesli, said they all sounded the same.

When I explained that he had to imagine the full swell of the band, he said it needed a miracle not imagination and he wouldn't be in it not if I paid him.

Miss Lane, the music teacher, who is really, really nice and goes out with the doctor (Shereen's mum told us) said to use what she calls pop tunes which would save me time and we all knew them already.

Everyone in the class agreed.

Butch Hills said it was a cop out and read the paper.

Gerald Tappering offered to lend me his record collection to choose tunes from. It is the best collection in the class but he was only trying to suck up after the row in the church.

I told him I'd borrow Shereen's collection which is the best in the school.

I am writing a lyric now for Buttercup the Mad Cow which is mega sad.

With love from your friend in England,
Anna Pitts

P.S. Shereen has just phoned from the disco and told Sis that it is not her fault about Andrew (oh, pain, pain!) and the deal to borrow her record collection is off. I have worked out that Buttercup the Mad Cow's lyric will fit to 'What Shall We Do With The Drunken Sailor', so all is not doom and gloom. A.P.

The Old Butcher's,
Leachfield,
Gloucestershire,
England,
The Planet

Tuesday March 14th

Dear Clare,

It will be better for me to stow away on a ship to Australia not an aeroplane because it is easier to lose oneself in the crowds on board ship. I will let you know when I am docking.

I have decided not to hang about saving money for a proper ticket but to leave home and my heartless family at once. Also the organic garden has given me chilblains.

James the chauffeur is in hospital.

On Sunday morning, there was a note stuffed in our letter box. It was written on a Kleenex tissue.

New Gran, who had driven down specially early to see Sis and Bunjie hunt, found it on her way in. It turns out she's been away all this time making a film in Africa. She threw the note in the Rayburn.

At breakfast, Sis was all dressed up in her new hunting gear except for her hat because Mum had still got to put her hair in a net which looks really strange. New Gran said it was a tragedy to push that glory of hair into a net.

And we all agreed.

Quite by accident, I dropped the marmalade in Sis's hat.

Sis swore.

New Gran shone really red through her tan and said I was a bad influence and I had given Sis swearing lessons. Then she told Mum she'd Rayburned a garish note to me about betting and booze to save Mum's feelings.

I ran to the Rayburn. Comme toujours, it had gone out overnight. The tissue was hot and sooty but there. Shereen had written on it in Beauty Without Cruelty's Red for Danger nail polish ANNA BET IT WAS GT.

You'd think even New Gran could figure out that gin and tonic is a G *and* T and GT is Gerald Tappering, who has outgrown his strength, and Shereen meant it was his fault about Andrew. And the pain.

But before I could put New Gran right, there was a bang on the front door and the Piranha careered in to say did we know her garden was full of revolting hens.

I said it was Ethel and not hens. The Piranha said whoever it was, it had ruined her garden.

It turns out the Piranha has been tending our garden and was fairly enraged to find we were using it.

I explained to the Piranha that Ethel's hobby is scratching and that was why she'd uprooted the new beech hedge that the Piranha had planted. But the Piranha did not get it.

Have you noticed how headstrong people are when they get off on a gardening kick? They are convinced the garden is only there for them to garden it.

The Piranha said hens were not for gardens but the dinner table, preferably as Chicken Kiev, which is surprising because the Piranha does not believe in Russia usually.

The Piranha said we did not appreciate her and New Gran said, 'That's right.'

And the Piranha smiled at New Gran and New Gran smiled at the Piranha and they both went up to the Piranha's flat for some Buck's Fizz which is an alcoholic breakfast drink of champagne and orange juice that James the chauffeur had made. Give it a miss. However much extra orange you add, you can't disguise that champagne taste.

Mum wiped out Sis's hat and said she was not all that keen on beech hedges.

I went to visit Ethel to boost her morale.

She was not there.

Only James the chauffeur was there.

I asked him if he had seen a hen. He said not to worry any more about the Piranha being upset by the hen. He'd got rid of it.

I remembered what the Piranha had said about dinner tables. I flew upstairs to her flat.

New Gran and the Piranha were lounging about drinking BF and listening to the Archers Omnibus.

The Piranha said, 'I hope you don't think I'm taking you to the Meet dressed like that, Anna.'

New Gran said, 'Hear hear.'

But I did not answer.

They are only jealous because Shereen has given me her mauve tulle mini that she has slimmed out of.

I ran into the kitchenette. There on the marble work top, cut in bits and well buttered, was the Piranha's chicken dinner.

I screamed, 'Ethel,' and tried to gather her up for a decent burial. She kept skidding out of my grip.

The Piranha came and asked if I'd gone mad and New Gran said, 'That child is disturbed.'

I said to the Piranha, 'You are a murdering, cannibalistic ratbag.' I ran downstairs with poor Ethel.

Mum was on the phone in the hall. 'Did you say ratbag?' I heard her ask. That Piranha moves like lightning.

James the chauffeur was still in the garden looking at Bunjie in his stable. Bunjie was wearing his best saddle with half his tail in a plait. They'd had to leave the other half unplaited. It was not worth the bloodshed.

I said to James, 'You are a fiend to perform such a wicked act for my grandmother.'

He laughed, yes, laughed, and said I would understand when I was a big girl which was strange because that is the put down adults use when they are boasting about their sexual know-how and I was talking murder.

Then he said, 'This pony's girth could be tighter.'
The girth is the belt Bunjie wears like this.

girth

'Shall I tighten it?' James asked.

Clare, I think and think about what happened next. James the chauffeur says now I didn't warn him but I really, really seem to remember I did.

He unlatched Bunjie's door and out leapt Bunjie. Crash went the door and sort of crushed James's finger between it and the wall. James yelled a mega swear.

Mum and Sis rushed out to catch Bunjie who was plunging about in the rest of the Piranha's beech hedge, and the Piranha and New Gran came sailing down to see what was happening.

And I took a spade and tried to find a quiet, respectful bit of the garden for the burial which was hard to do with everyone messing about in it.

The Piranha bandaged James's finger with her hanky. Then the Piranha ran to fetch her car to drive James to hospital.

And New Gran said she would take the rest of us to the Meet and ran into the shed we call our garage for her Vauxhall. And I got down to digging.

Mum kept calling to me to help catch Bunjie and not to worry at the moment about repairing the damage Ethel had done to the Piranha's garden.

Mum can't half get hold of the wrong end of the stick. I gave her a forgiving wave and dug on.

The Piranha backed her car into the garden and New Gran backed hers out of the shed and they backed, crump, into each other.

The Piranha shouted, 'Now look what you've done, you painted road hog!'

And New Gran hissed, 'Vous êtes ivres!' Which was French so Sis wouldn't understand.

I have looked up ivres, in the French dictionary. It is drunk. I have told Sis.

Then New Gran and the Piranha tried to get their cars away from each other. Their engines roared and roared but they were locked back to back.

The Piranha went round and shouted through New Gran's window, 'Rev, you geriatric bimbo!' And New Gran wagged her finger at the Piranha and said, 'Temper, temper.'

The Piranha pelted back to her car rather stormily and really put her foot down. There was like a giant feedback noise. New Gran squealed and jumped out just as her exhaust system came away on the Rover's rear bumper.

The Rover shot forward at many miles an hour and James the chauffeur dived gymnastically out of its path into Bunjie's stable.

Sadly though, he hadn't noticed the door had swung shut again.

Quelle wallop!

The Piranha raced on up the garden with New Gran's exhaust pipes ploughing a big rut in her lawn, I'm afraid, until she pulled up with a crackle in the last of her beech hedge.

Not one of them noticed New Gran's Vauxhall rolling away all by itself until it wedged its nose in our back door very loudly. Clouds of our house rose up but at least it did not fall down.

And it was a good thing really because it caught Bunjie's interest so Mum and Sis could grab him, and at last peace and quiet reigned in our garden.

The Ethel bits were in the hole I'd dug. I had tried to wipe the corpse clean but lulls don't necessarily last long in our family so I'd decided to hurry and bury her buttery.

Do you know that beautiful hymn, 'There is a Green Hill'? I was singing it feelingly – and suddenly everyone except James, who was out for the count, started screaming at me that it was all my fault.

It is so typical of my family to interrupt a funeral.

Then the Piranha said, 'My God! That child is actually burying my Sunday dinner,' and they all screamed again.

New Gran took hold of my spade to unbury Ethel but I hung on to the shovel end. We were having a sort of tug of war with it when I heard this unearthly clucking.

At first I thought it was Ethel calling up to me from below – like Hamlet's Dad, the Spook, does – to be revenged on the Piranha and James and the rest of my family. Anyway, I let go of my end of the spade.

Unfortunately, New Gran was still pulling her end v. heartily and so she went running backwards with it till she sat down with a slurp noise right in Bunjie's manure heap and her suede trousers were a write-off.

I looked over our garden wall and there was Ethel sitting in the field with – wait for it – *three* eggs.

I was really, really happy because it was better than Lazarus even who miraculously jumped out of his grave after he was certified dead and gone and went on to live the life of a normal man.

But my family would not share my joy.

The ambulance came and carried James the chauffeur away.

He has a broken finger. Also a tooth.

We missed the Meet.

Sis cried.

The AA came for New Gran's car.

The RAC came for the Piranha's.

The Builders said they would come to fix the back door. But they didn't.

The police came. They'd heard there had been an incident.

The Piranha and New Gran are not speaking.

Sis is not speaking.

No one is speaking.

I am not speaking.

I dug up the Piranha's Chicken Kiev and put it back in her kitchenette but she is still not speaking.

I offered New Gran my Australia fare money for a new pair of trousers but she said she'd rather I used it to go to Australia.

Mum has not noticed I am not speaking and keeps asking me questions. I am aching to remind her about her bike and Wednesdays. But I don't.

She does not notice I don't answer.

I bet she won't notice when I've gone to Australia.

None of them will notice.

107

Sis has just pushed a note under my door but I shall ignore it.

With love from your friend in England,
Anna Pitts

P.S. The note says Gerald Tappering has come to see me and is waiting downstairs. Sis is a really pathetic liar even in note form. A.P.

P.P.S. I wish Gainsborough could speak. A.P.

The Old Butcher's,
Leachfield,
Gloucestershire,
England,
The Planet

Friday March 17th

Dear Clare,

Would you believe, Mr Bull, the reporter, has a son? He is eighteen and called Quentin.

Yesterday, the widow of one of the Piranha's ex-husbands came to collect her Daimler and she collected James the chauffeur too. He has been convalescing with the Piranha for a few days.

The Piranha said she'd go along as well to help nurse the gap in his front teeth.

Mum was v. surprised. She starts work stencilling the chicken farm next Monday and the Piranha was going to look after the gallery while Mum was out.

Mum and the Piranha had a row.

Sis and me heard it.

We had to.

I expect you heard it in Narrowmine, Queensland, Australia.

Mum won on points but the Piranha still went with James.

Quentin is waiting for the next stage in his life to happen so until it occurs, Mr Bull has lent him to us to look after our gallery.

Mum has to leave him his meals.

He is a vegetarian.

He starts on Monday.

Today, I checked out if he liked pasta. He said, 'Yeh.'

Phew! Phew!

Quentin looks exactly like Mr Bull only smooth. Also Quentin's hair is a real colour and not grey.

Bob the gamekeeper has found Bunjie a paddock to spend the day in. We draw lots each day for who is to take him to it. It is a high risk trip. Yesterday, Mum lost.

The paddock belongs to the doctor who goes out with Miss Lane, the music teacher. He talks to you in jokes because you are a kid but he bandaged Mum's arm most professionally. And this morning he was in here bright and early to check it out before surgery.

It turns out Gerald Tappering was really downstairs. He stayed for one hour waiting for me.

Mum found him sitting in the dark in the hall. He handed her a Madonna video he wanted to lend me (which is a dead loss because we haven't got a video player) and went home.

Mum gave me a really serious talk about rudeness and selfishness and arrogance and coquettishness and unkindness, which was v. unfair of her because as I am not speaking, I had forfeited my right to reply.

Mum packed it in much sooner than usual though.

Maybe not answering is the way to handle serious talks. Have you tried that with Mrs Hannock, your mum?

I broke my vow of silence to tell Sis I would kill her at the first opportunity.

I returned the Madonna video yesterday during break and told Gerald Tappering how rude and selfish and arrogant and unkind it was of him to presume we had a video player.

He seemed truly repentant so then I asked him if it was true what Shereen had written about him on the Kleenex.

Oh Clare, I can hardly bear to write this but as we swore to tell all in our letters, I will.

Two weeks, one hour and twenty minutes ago, I was in town in Halfords buying Mum's Mother's Day present which is the pad bit to fix the front brake on her bike because I know she really, really wants that so I can borrow it on Wednesdays.

I went round the shelves looking for the brakes section and suddenly, bang in front of me, at the motor bike accessories, was Andrew.

Time stood still.

He looked up.

He saw me.

He smiled.

I held on to the shelves. A bottle of chrome polish wobbled and fell over.

He leaned across and stood it up.

He uses Brute.

110

He said, 'Hello, Anna.' And, oh Clare, why, oh why, oh why, oh why did I do it? I said, 'Anthea.'

He said, 'Your friend said your name was Anna.'

I hoped it was just that my glasses had steamed up because he went misty but it crossed my mind I might be going to have hysterics. Forever.

Then I thought of Kylie Minogue and what she would have done so I let go of the shelf.

I put one hand on my waist and the other in my jeans pocket. It wouldn't quite go in because my jeans have become rather tight but after a completely unnoticeable shove, in it went and I gave him the engaging smile I have been practising.

It is open and honest and yet alluring. He seemed to find it pretty fascinating.

And I said, 'Let's let Anthea be our name.'

And he said, 'Ok, Anna.' And went out of Halfords.

And a voice behind me said in a squeaky, stupid way, 'Let's let Anthea be our name.' And there was that Butch Hills with the face like a plate of muesli.

I could have died.

I picked up Mum's brake pad and walked to the cash desk loftily. When I came to get my money out I found that my hand had become trapped inside my jeans pocket. I explained to the queue behind me that my money was stuck with my hand in my jeans pocket and made a little jest about a tight fit and tight fisted.

But they were not strong on humour.

I tried to lever my hand out with my free hand. My elbow jabbed the old man behind me in the chest. He said he had fought the war for me.

I asked the girl on the till if there was somewhere

I could take my jeans off to release my cash. She said, 'This is Halfords, not a strip joint.' A man further back in the queue asked me why I didn't get lost.

I left Halfords and the brake pad in a dignified fashion.

Butch Hills has got a really uninfectious laugh.

I wandered the shopping precinct in black despair. The ladies toilets were closed for de-vandalisation so I didn't get my hand out of my pocket till Miss Selfridge's changing room. All the blood had gone from it.

I thought maybe I will get terminal gangrene. And Andrew will place flowers on Halfords motor bike accessories shelf every year in my memory. But so far no luck.

I love Andrew so much I could fill the whole page with Andrew Andrew Andrew Andrew Andrew Andrew Andrew. But how can he return the love of a girl who doesn't know her own name?

So

I have decided we must never meet again. He may find it hard to understand at first but later he will come to see it is the best thing for both of us.

R.I.P.

Butch Hills has been away from school since the Halfords incident with a grave case of flu so it's true: there is a God.

Yesterday, Gerald Tappering confessed to me that he told Andrew my real name so it wasn't Shereen after all. As we are Auriol's chief bridesmaids, it is useful we are speaking again.

Gerald told Andrew at youth club. Andrew goes to youth club nearly every week.

It is in Bamford.

On Wednesdays.

With love from your friend in Love and in England,

Anna Pitts

P.S. I have bought a bottle of Brute. I take little sniffs to help me through this weary life.

I couldn't afford Mum's Mother's Sunday present after that so I have promised her two next year. I will send them from Australia so what she loses now, she will make up for in novelty. Also, it will help her notice I have left home. A.P.

P.P.S. Mum has bought a new pad and fixed the front brake on her bike so now I can borrow it to get to youth club in Bamford on Wednesday nights. A.P.

The Old Butcher's,
Leachfield,
Gloucestershire,
England,
The Planet

Saturday March 18th

Dear Clare,

7 a.m.

There aren't any serious boats to Australia. They

113

are for holiday makers and dawdle all round the seas. The last one went in January and the next one doesn't go till November.

I shall have to stow away on a plane which will be more of a challenge to secrete Ethel and Gainsborough.

Sis is having another go at hunting today.

It turns out we were all getting ready on the wrong day last weekend. Daisy, Sis's friend, said nobody hunts on a Sunday.

I pointed out to my relatives that I had saved the family dignity. But for my mistake about Ethel and the Chicken Kiev, Sis would have been tally-hoing solo round the countryside looking a wally.

But they did not get it.

Mum says I can borrow her bike when I've finished at the organic garden and try to catch them up.

New Gran has hired a sweet little Fiesta car.

8 a.m.

That doctor may be a joker but he is v. serious about doctoring. He has just called in again to check Mum's arm.

4 p.m.

I caught up with the hunt.

I saw the fox.

I am joining the saboteurs' club.

6:15 p.m.

Bunjie has just been brought home. V. v. muddy. After Sis fell off him for the third time, he must have decided to strike out on his own. No one knows where he has been.

It is strange to think of Bunjie having a private life.

We rang the police to tell them to call off the search. They are very good at being police here. They can detect Mum's voice as soon as she speaks now.

7:30 p.m.

I have only this minute finished cleaning up Bunjie. He was so tired he couldn't even be bothered to bite me.

Sis is lying down waiting for her witch hazel to take effect on her bruises.

Not a rumour of tea.

Typical Mum.

9:30 p.m.

Quelle Family Row!

At 8:45 p.m. we sat down to a gourmet tea of bread and cheese. Sis had to sit on a tepid hot-water bottle for her bruises which is the nearest thing we could think of to a rubber ring. Then New Gran, who is down for the weekend, comme toujours, said with a smile that Sis's dad, the stunt man, had sent Mum thousands of dollars all the way from LA.

'YEH!!!!' went Sis and me but Mum was really quiet for someone who has just hit the jackpot.

Not to seem ungrateful to New Gran, I sketched in a few of the little luxuries we could splash out on with our new found wealth – e.g. recycled toilet paper, a back door, and a tranquillizing gun for Bunjie. Plus, an outright cash payment to each member of the family – i.e. my fare to come and live with you in Australia.

New Gran said, 'Actually, dear, the money is for your sister to go to boarding school with her little friend Daisy.'

Have you ever had that wish for the ground to open and take you away from a situation?

As it didn't, I read the Kraft cheese slice packet many times.

Mum said over and over that the school in disguise as a castle was against her beliefs.

New Gran said you could take GCSEs in riding at the castle.

I asked what use just one GCSE was going to be to Bunjie. New Gran went very red and tore her bread into sixths and said I was holding Sis back.

Sis cried.

Mum said, 'Holding her back from what?'

Then New Gran tore her bread again and again so it was unusable, and gave this totally false description of me. How I had made a scene today at the hunt and shown them up, how I went about with young criminals, and received notes about drinking and gambling, and how I sniffed Brute, how I gave Sis swearing lessons and had no dress sense and put about mendacious (whatever that is) reports of my sexual activities and behaved irrationally with pasta and jointed chicken and the repairs to her car would cost £900.

Secretly, I sometimes wonder if New Gran did lose her husband. I think it is more likely he ran away. As fast as his legs would carry him. But that is just between you and me.

As we were really talking about Sis and not me

I only said comfortingly that the estimate for her car was £893 not £900. And New Gran said, 'See what I mean, see what I mean.'

Sis cried louder.

I said I agreed Sis should go to boarding school because then I could use her bedroom as the operational headquarters for my Anti Blood Sport campaign.

Sis stopped crying to say no I couldn't.

Mum said it was dividing our family and out of the question. New Gran said she had grandparent's rights. Mum threw the washing up at the sink.

New Gran said my school was a sump of feeble-minded louts. It is amazing when you think that New Gran has never actually met Butch Hills with the face like a plate of muesli, that she could come up with that bull's-eye description.

Mum dented the bread board.

Mum said the castle school was full of over privileged pea brains. Which sounds as if Sis would fit in really nicely, so – own goal, Mum.

New Gran said she thought we should hear what Sis had to say about it.

Sis cried.

We all listened politely to Sis crying.

I made us all a coffee while we waited for her to deliver. New Gran said Sis was crying because she so desperately wanted to go to boarding school.

It turned out she had fallen off her hot-water bottle.

To lighten the atmosphere, I quipped that if Sis couldn't stay on a hot-water bottle it was going to be a long haul to learn to stay on Bunjie and maybe

Sis's dad should budget for extra time at the castle school.

We had lift off!

Mum shouted that I was no help and lost her grip on the Branston pickle. Quelle yuk!

New Gran went Poppy Day red and tore off this stunning jacket she has with huge, huge shoulder pads and shouted, 'See what I mean, see what I mean.'

Sis upped her volume three decibels.

Just then, in came Auriol and Shereen with my bridesmaid's dress and Shereen's mum came too because she is making the dresses and everybody had to stop quarrelling and pretend to be dead friendly and evacuate the kitchen so we wouldn't get the dresses pickly.

And New Gran said she had never seen anything like the apricot with the coffee trimmings and when I saw myself in the mirror I had to agree.

It is the nicest I have ever looked.

With love from your friend in England,
Anna Pitts

P.S. I have looked up mendacious in the dictionary. It is a liar. That New Gran certainly comes out with some really spiteful statements. How can she say I lie about my sexual activities when she knows I don't have any?

But time cures all. Phew! Phew! A.P.

The Old Butcher's,
Leachfield,
Gloucestershire,
England,
The Planet

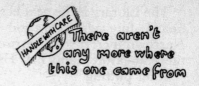
HANDLE WITH CARE
There aren't any more where this one came from

March 20th

Dear Clare,

Mr Bull's son, Quentin started work today. He sold a chest of drawers worth £250. Which was great except he sold it for £2.50.

Mum told him to go and wait for the next stage in his life somewhere else as far away from her as possible.

I was really looking forward to having another vegetarian in the house.

I think Mum's arm must be critical. The doctor calls twice a day to check it.

Carol on the bus said they are turning kangaroos into leather handbags in Rome. Please check out that repugnant fact at once. If true, you and me can take Global Action.

Mum said the Piranha will definitely come back and mind the gallery when she hears how Quentin has lost Mum £247.50 and she will phone her in the cheap time.

It is really hard to find a hunt saboteurs' cell. At the dentist's, the receptionist told me they were bringing back hanging for hunt saboteurs which was a bit of a worry.

I got the feeling from her that saboteurs lie low in Polytechnics and Squats but we do not have either of those in Leachfield.

The Library is the next best thing. It has a notice board for ads. Do you have a library in Narrowmine? If so advertise for help with foiling the Kangaroo Hand Bag Hunters.

I am putting

SCHOOL GIRL WISHES MEET HUNT SABOTEUR WITH A VIEW TO ASSISTING WITH DEEDS BELOW AGE OF IMPRISONMENT SO USEFUL FRONTLINE WORKER. REPLIES PLEASE TO:— MISS A. PITTS THE OLD BUTCHERS, LEACHFIELD GLOUCESTERSHIRE, ENGLAND The Planet

KEEP BLOOD OUT OF SPORT

That will flush out an accomplice or so into the open.

You can copy mine if you like. Change your decoration from vixens/foxes and cubs to kangaroos. I tried one but the pouches are murder to get to look right.

Sis said the fox enjoyed being hunted.

120

I asked her where she'd met the fox that told her that.

She said it was my turn to fetch Bunjie from the doctor's paddock.

Mum said in a morbid sort of voice that she would go for him even though it wasn't her turn.

Sis and I decided the loss of £247.50 has disturbed the balance of her mind.

Sis said she would make the supper for Mum while she was out to cheer her up.

Bob, the gamekeeper, came to help put Ethel to bed. He did not stay for his boxed wine. He gave us a Mars bar and asked us if we missed our dad. I said, 'Which one?' But he didn't seem to understand. He left Mum a present.

It is another eel.

We divided the Mars bar. Sis did first cut. I had first choice.

The phone rang. It was the Piranha. At Heathrow.

She was just about to board a flight to Turkey for a little holiday with James the chauffeur.

I started to tell her about Quentin and the chest of drawers.

Her money ran out.

We were cut off.

We decided to toss a coin for who was to break the Turkey news to Mum. We looked in Mum's purse for a 10p. It was empty.

We hid the eel.

We waited for Mum.

I went up to the Piranha's flat and borrowed a bottle of her brandy. We put it on standby for medicinal purposes.

Then we waited for Mum.

She did not come.

We rang the police and reported Mum missing.

We ate the supper Sis had made. We put Mum's to one side.

The doctor called up to say Mum and Bunjie were having dinner with him.

We tipped Mum's supper back in the cornflake packet.

The sergeant was really nice when we rang the police and reported Mum found. He said the Gloucestershire Constabulary would feel quite underworked without a member of our family to search for.

Sorry, it's Tuesday 21st now, 9:30 p.m.

Everybody in my class thought my musical *Arable Agony* was going to be great. Our final script conference with Miss Lane the music teacher, who goes out with the doctor, was scheduled for today.

Butch Hills was back from the flu. He said Arable A. was rubbish. By the end of the conference, most of the class had gone over to his side.

Miss Lane asked everyone what part they would like to play and there was a big silence. At last, Gerald Tappering who has outgrown his strength, said he would be Buttercup the Mad Cow but he was only sucking up after the row about the video player. Quelle creep!

Anyway, I thought I would be best as the cow. For once, Butch Hills agreed with me.

Miss Lane said we ought to start by appointing a director before the Easter holidays begin this

Thursday and as Butch Hills had strong views on the casting, he would be good as the director.

But even Butch Hills could see that was the old 'make the Bolshie one boss' child psychiatry routine that they all are fed when they are being drilled as teachers, and he said no way.

So we left it. And that is the end of *Arable Agony*.

After that, Miss Lane made us learn this really difficult song. She went on and on till we got it right. A new song right at the end of term, would you believe!

The words were unusually old fashioned for Miss Lane too. All about how really great love is to start with and then it wears out.

As the doctor is so v. cheerful, I hope when she goes out with him, Miss Lane does not show this mopey side of her nature or it may not last.

Shereen has just rung. She says Butch Hills has put it round the school that I am a schizoid nut case and would I look up schizoid in the dictionary for her.

It is a split personality.

She wondered how he had thought up such a weird insult. Halfords is how and this Anthea I am stuck with.

Shereen said not to worry as me having two personalities put me two up on Butch.

Sometimes you realise what friends are for. Even second best ones.

I've just had this idea for a one girl show about factory farming.

Mum's been in to say I should have an early night after yesterday evening's carry on. Sis and me were still waiting for Mum when Mr Bull the reporter came running in with a cheque for her for £247.50 to make up for Quentin's mistake.

I told him Mum was at the doctor's.

He said he hoped it was nothing serious.

I said it was dinner.

Mr Bull gave me that loopy stare that makes me worry he is not all there.

He asked us did we miss our dad.

I turned on the television.

The three of us were all watching this really good film when Bob the gamekeeper came back. When he saw Mr Bull, he said, 'What's this then?'

But Sis said, 'Sh.' So we all four watched the film.

When the ads came on, we gave them the box of wine to drink but there wasn't much left so it was a good thing I had borrowed the Piranha's brandy.

After the film was over, Mr Bull said he would do anything for Mum, and Bob said he would too.

Then Mr Bull said he thought he would do anything for Mum much better than Bob would do it.

And Bob said, no, he would.

Then they both said it all over again. Twice.

By now it was really boring and late so Sis and me told them we had school tomorrow and to turn out the lights and drop the Yale latch when they left and we went up to bed.

Mum said, when she came in from the doctor's, they were both asleep with their heads on the kitchen table. She propped a note against the empty brandy bottle asking them to turn out the lights and drop the Yale latch when they left and she went to bed.

You'd think after all that, they would have

remembered to turn out the lights and drop the Yale latch when they left.

Last night, Sis asked me if I missed my dad, John, the art student. I told her you cannot miss someone you do not know.

She said New Gran was fixing for her to go to Hollywood to meet her dad. I told her that made her one step nearer missing him.

And Sis said, 'Oh, but my dad is not a bus.'

That is Sis's idea of a joke!

I know there is Life After Sis but sometimes I think I shall be dead of her terrible jokes by the time I get there and I will not be able to enjoy it.

Well, well! What with the Piranha in Turkey and Sis going to Hollywood and me going to Australia, we shall be a much travelled family.

Poor old Mum. Stuck in Leachfield. Stencilling an egg farm.

Today, I asked Mum to buy a water filter jug so Sis and me would not be poisoned with nitrates.

She said no.

The doctor called to re-dress Mum's Bunjie wounds.

Mum told him she always put her children first.

Sis cried.

I asked Mum to buy us a water filter jug so Sis and me would not be poisoned with nitrates.

She said no.

I went for a mirthless laugh and to feed Gainsborough.

With love from your friend in England,
Anna Pitts
P.S. Sis reckons Bob the gamekeeper fancies

Mum and wants to marry her. I don't know where Sis gets these ideas. A.P.

P.P.S. I have found out where. New Gran. A.P.

P.P.P.S. Sis says New Gran said Mr Bull the reporter wants to too. Personally, I cannot imagine anyone wanting to marry Mum. Also her track record proves this. But there you are. It takes all sorts to make a world/planet. A.P.

To:-
The Prime Minister,
10, Downing Street,
London,
England,
The Planet

March 22nd

Dear Prime Minister,

A short note on the subject of wind.

What has everyone got against it? Why the lousy image?

Oil is coming to an end.
Coal is coming to an end.
Gas is coming to an end.

Good riddance, say some, because all three are such pollutants that

The Planet is coming to an end

But you must be worried stiff because you say, we all know in our heart of hearts we must have energy for our markets to grow.

I think of you roving the corridors of number 10, Downing Street, and Chequers at the weekends, in quest of an answer.

And here it is right under our noses. Wind. Wind without end. It's so obvious once you've thought of it, isn't it?

Please order lots and lots of windmills that will supply hundreds of kilowatts of squeaky clean electricity to all and sundry.

That way, you will be the first leader to leap free of their Windist Shackles. And the Planet will take one step back from its polluted doom.

But wait, I hear you say. What about our cars? We can't put them under sail. And although it would look very pretty because everyone could have their own colours and patterns, I have to agree.

Imagine a busy thoroughfare like the M25 on a calm day. Everyone just sitting there not able to budge. Except my grandmother says that is not a good example because that is what they do now with engines.

Well, as two heads are better than one, I leave that problem with you to work out.

Yours sincerely,
Anna Pitts
Aged 13 years

The Old Butcher's
Leachfield,
Gloucestershire,
England,
The Planet

March 23rd

Dear Clare,

I have been to Youth Club. It is wonderful.

At first it was v. ordinary because it was mostly kids from school. No Butch Hills though. Phew! Phew! It is too far for him to come.

I had to sit in the toilet for a long time waiting for my sweat to dry. Mum's bike is a killer. But I came out still damp because the toilet has spiders.

Westlow, whose father the stockman will pulverise him, showed me how to play pool and said he would like to be Buttercup the Mad Cow, in *Arable Agony*.

I told him *Arable Agony* is now a one girl show called *Deadly Nitrates*. And it is the story of a beautiful, poor orphan girl who converts a young, rich, handsome, proud farmer to see that he is poisoning the earth and water with chemicals and together, they go organic.

Westlow said it did not sound as much fun as Buttercup the Mad Cow but that is his problem. Then Gerald Tappering came and played pool too and asked me to go to confirmation classes with him. He explained they are like GCSE for Christians and at the end you get a white dress.

I told him I would read the Bible and think about it but I could not picture him in a white dress.

He said he would pray for me.

Then they all started to discuss this charity fund-raising thing. The idea is, we split into groups and each group builds something that floats and then we race them on the Bourne where it is too shallow to drown us and get sponsors to pay us for how long we stay afloat.

Then they chose captains and the captains chose teams. They started to discuss plans.

And so I got ready to go home.

Andrew came in.

I sank into a seat.

Unfortunately, there was not one quite there so I sat rather hard on the floor but I tried to make it look as natural as possible.

Everyone wanted Andrew in their team. Andrew said he wanted to be a captain. They said there wasn't any crew left for him. He said, 'What's wrong with our Miss Pitts?'

My heart sang.

I tried to stand.

I didn't make it.

Then Gerald Tappering said he would change to Andrew's team.

I did not care.

Then Westlow said that he would too. I gave a gracious smile but as I have not practised it, I am not sure how it came out.

Andrew is coming to build our craft in Westlow's garden on Easter Sunday. Two and a Half Days To Wait.

Cycling home it was v. dark. The front lamp kept going on and off like it was signalling for help. Also my legs had put on weight. The bike was so heavy

I began to think I had picked up the wrong one. I had to stop whistling in the end because I could not spare the air.

Do you have street lamps in Narrowmine, Queensland, Australia?

A great thing fluttered and flipped over my head. I ducked.

I fell off the bike.

Of course, it was an owl or some such night-life but it is hard not to make the decision it is a ghost even when you do not believe in them.

I told God I really, truthfully would read the Bible if he got me home in return. And I set off again.

Then I saw a car's lights coming towards me. Then the car stopped just ahead of me. It was taking up the whole width of the lane. I was caught in its lights. I rushed on and scraped past it.

But it began driving backwards to catch up with me. I was so scared, I suddenly could pedal really hard but the car kept coming backwards and backwards after me. I was going at top speed. But it drew level with me. I went up on the verge. My light went out.

Then Mum's voice shouted at me to stop and it was Mum in her car.

I was really, really angry with her.

I told her how she had nearly scared me to death and how I'd thought she was a child molester and what a pathetic front lamp she had on her bike and how she never thought about me at all or my feelings.

And Mum screamed at me how dare I go riding about in the dark by myself and how many times had she told me.

And I screamed how I'd said to her again and again I was going to Youth Club and she hadn't objected.

And she screamed I hadn't told her and she'd wormed it out of Sis.

And I screamed the sooner Sis went to boarding school, the better.

And we were screaming at each other by the lights of Mum's car when another car came along and stopped and it was the Chicken Farmer. He asked, could he help, and Mum said, 'It's all right, John, (I told you everyone is called John) 'it's only Anna.'

Although I did not mean them to, the tears came out of my eyes. They put me in Mum's car.

Then they tried to put the bike in with me but neither me nor the bike were supple enough. As they were trying to stuff it in on top of me, the Chicken Farmer began to laugh a bit, I think, so I was really glad when quite by accident, Mum trod on his foot and he stopped laughing and said, 'Ouch!'

That's one for the poor little chickens, I thought to myself.

At last, he got the idea to put the bike in his Volvo which is the size of a deep litter free range shed anyway and he took the bike and dropped it off at home for us.

Mum came and sat in the car and gave me tissues and a hug and I gave her a hug to show I did not bear her a grudge for giving me a nervous breakdown. And then she said running off into the dark was not going to stop Sis going to boarding school.

She seemed to expect me to disagree but only a seriously impaired person could have done that.

Sometimes I really don't know where to start with Mum. I was pushed for an answer.

I said nothing.

Then she remarked that once she had been a teenager. Mum sometimes comes out with these things right out of the blue. Does Mrs Hannock do that? Anyway, as we were getting along so cosily, I just said I was sorry to hear that.

I have since worked out that Mum was a teenager a whole fifth of a century ago when life was simple. For us present day ones, the minute we blow out the thirteenth candle on our cake – we hit white water.

When we stayed at a hotel for Christmas, they left out bedroom number thirteen. They jumped straight from number twelve to fourteen so no one would have to sleep in an unlucky number bedroom.

Maybe they should do that for teenagers. Maybe if they started us off at fourteen years and cut out the unlucky thirteen the whole History of Teenagers would be a v. rosier story. Except we would miss a birthday.

Then Mum told me that Sis was going to the castle private school for an experiment. I said I hadn't realised they went in for vivisection up there. Mum didn't get it.

I told her not to worry. With me being a teenager now, I was probably hard to understand.

She said nothing.

We made a pact that I would always ask for a lift to Youth Club even though it is not so good for the ecology.

On the way home, Mum asked me who was at Youth Club.

I said, 'Nobody much.'

I did not want to seem uninterested so I asked her what she had been doing that evening.

She said, 'Nothing much.'

With love from your friend in England,
Anna Pitts

The Old Butcher's,
Leachfield,
Gloucestershire,
England,
The Planet

Good Friday. One and a half days to ANDREW

Dear Clare,

Because of the cheque, Mr Bull the reporter's son, Quentin, has been allowed back to mind the gallery which is un peu boring because now the holidays have started, I have to mind him to make sure he does not do a chest of drawers again.

Also he does not wear Brute.

And take it from me, he should.

Still no contact from the hunt saboteurs. Have you had any luck with the Kangaroo hand bags?

The receptionist at the dentist said hunt saboteurs should be horse whipped and put in the stocks. I did not disagree as they have ways of getting back at you at the dentist.

This morning, at breakfast, there were no hot cross buns.

Typical Mum.

Sis cried.

I told her, according to all the books I'd read on the subject of boarding schools, girls there do not cry on pain of direst death.

New Gran, who is down for the weekend, comme toujours, and Bank Holiday Monday as well, said I was silly and that Sis was sensitive, like her dad.

Mum agreed that sensitivity was a quality Sis's dad shared with the ox.

I grabbed Sis and we cleared out fast but we could still hear them from right up the garden by the Piranha's dead beech hedge.

Sis said she was proud of her dad being like an ox because they were v. strong.

I could have done with fetching a pencil from indoors to draw diagrams with. It is easier to explain to Sis how an ox gets to become so strong with the help of pictures because Sis does not understand words like doctored. Well, she thinks it's one of Snow White's seven dwarfs.

But I could tell by the racket, the house was still a No Go area so I did my best without.

Sis just about got the idea, I think, by the time New Gran came haring out on all cylinders and swept her off to shop for Easter eggs.

This was a shame because it was Sis's turn for the Bunjie run to the doctor's paddock and I had to take him instead. On the way, he bit me in the waist. To pay him back, I broke the news to him that he is going on a big hunt on Monday.

There was a car parked by the paddock gate. To my surprise, there was Miss Lane, the music teacher, sitting at the wheel.

Isn't it weird how different teachers seem in the

holidays? She was dressed like she was just off to a party. Except for the wellingtons.

Miss Lane asked me how my mother was.

I said she was ok.

Then she asked where my mother was.

I said she was working for the chicken farmer's wife who looks like a model and rides side-saddle at the hunt.

After that there was a lull in the conversation.

I tried to think of something musical to say but it is hard to do when you are bleeding from the waist.

She offered me a sweet.

It turned out to be an aniseed ball.

I hate aniseed.

I swallowed it whole for politeness.

I choked. Terminally.

All of a sudden, cool as a cucumber, I had this entire plan in my head for sabotaging the hunt. While I was choking to death, I was visited with it.

It seemed really unfair that I was going to die of choking before I had a chance to put my plan into operation but fortunately, Miss Lane hit me so hard on the back, the aniseed ball flew out and stuck in Bunjie's mane, and my life was saved.

And Bunjie kicked Miss Lane.

I suggested she drove round the corner to the doctor's to have it bandaged and she gave a wild sort of laugh. I did not get it but I laughed too to keep her company.

Miss Lane gave me a lift to Bamford.

I went to the paper shop. Carol from the school bus works there in the holidays.

We collected up all the bags of aniseed balls they

had on the display and a whole big boxful more from out the back.

They were un peu expensive. I put them on Mum's paper bill. I will get a Saturday job straight away in Australia and send the money back to her.

Is school free in Australia?

If not, I shall have to give it up young.

I took the short cut home. You wouldn't believe how heavy aniseed balls weigh.

Mum was on countdown at the gallery door because I was not there to Quentin-sit.

The bottom fell out of my box. All the aniseed packets hit the gallery floor.

One burst open. Mum went into free fall.

Aniseed balls rolled all over.

It is a well-known fact that I hate aniseed.

Quelle miracle! Mum's interrogation was interrupted. The gallery door bell rang and Mum was grounded. We were both on instant smile for that rare species – a customer.

Saved by the bell. Jape, jape.

It was only Quentin arriving late for work but by then Mum had run out of steam and belted off to work at the chicken farm.

Quelle narrow squeak! Sweat! Sweat!

Quentin and me settled down for the morning. I asked him if he was ok.

He said, 'Yeh.'

At eleven o'clock, I asked him if he'd like a coffee.

He said, 'Yeh.'

At one o'clock, I asked him if he'd like some pasta.

He said, 'Yeh.'

We shut the gallery and ate the spaghetti Mum

had left for him. He went to sleep. I guess he'd OD'd on conversation.

I wish he would use Brute.

I set to work on the aniseed balls.

It is my plan to crush them all to a powder and scatter some powder where the hunt meets. Unlike me, hounds love aniseed more than anything else in the world. I will lay a trail of aniseed across country and all the hounds will run after my trail instead of the fox. And the hunt will ride after the hounds as usual. And everyone will have an ace time as usual. Only this time, so will the fox family who can stay at home, messing about in their den etc.

It is really hard to crush an aniseed ball with Mum's rolling pin. By the end of the dinner hour, I had done five.

Gerald Tappering rang.

He asked me to go to this church service tonight where they put all the lights out.

Quelle crudité!

I said no.

He asked me to come to confirmation class with him.

I said I might if he'd come and help me crush aniseed balls.

He rang off.

Sorry, it's Saturday now – one day to ANDREW

This morning, Mum had a letter from the bank and Mr Bull the reporter's cheque for £247.50 was in it marked re-present which means it has bounced.

Mum went from 0–60 mph in two seconds flat. Then she called Mr Bull the reporter.

Sadly, she strangled an important bit of the phone

during her conversation and we cannot telephone out any more. Still, it saves on the phone bill.

When Quentin arrived for work, Mum sent him away which was really, really mean of her because I'd got Easter Saturday off from work at Will and Belinda's but now I'm minding the gallery.

I said it was child, slave labour.

Mum promised to pay me but haggled over what was a living wage.

As usual Mum won. But only in the mind.

She rushed off with Bunjie to the doctor's paddock. As they disappeared out of sight, I saw her just get her elbow out of reach of Bunjie's teeth. I felt really mean that I was sorry to see that.

Sis is not here.

New Gran brought her back yesterday with an Easter egg that took up the whole of the back seat of the Fiesta. (Poor old New Gran still hasn't had any joy from the Piranha's insurance company about paying for the repairs to the Vauxhall.) She was très red right down her neck in a V-shape as far as you could see. She said she was taking Sis to a hotel. Mum said let's all go for dinner for a treat.

New Gran pointed. She wears this really beautiful, bronze nail polish with incorporated glitter.

'Viper!' She said.

I looked round, thinking she was warning me we had got one in our kitchen. Believe it or not, she was pointing at me.

Mum sighed and said, 'Now what?'

Sis cried.

Then New Gran said that I'd told Sis her dad

138

was a eunuch. Sadly, my dictionary was upstairs.

Mum said Sis should be able to work out that her dad couldn't be a eunuch and got a pencil and paper to show her.

New Gran gave a snort. Yes, really, a snort. I have never heard anyone do that before and off they went to a hotel. With the egg.

When Sis went up to pack, she asked me to come and help decide which was her comb but really it was to ask me what a eunuch was.

She had this idea it was a foreign football event. I told her I did not think that would rate immediate evacuation and I'd research it. She said she'd save me a bit of the egg.

I have looked up eunuch in the dictionary which was hard to do because unexpectedly it does not start with a U.

It is a castrated man. They are obsolete now.

I cannot think where Sis picks up these ideas. I must stop and ring her at the hotel to deliver the eunuch info or she will let us in for another of Mum's illustrated biology lessons.

With love from your friend in England,
Anna Pitts

P.S. Quentin came back with a cheque for £247.50 signed by Mrs Sally Bull. I asked him if it would bounce. He seemed to put up a real struggle for mouth control. But then he shrugged. Then he went to sleep by the till so I had to let him stay. I think I might have to tell him about Brute. A.P.

P.P.S. Can't phone Sis. Mum's done the phone in. A.P.

P.P.P.S. Ethel's laid another two eggs. Just in

139

time for Easter. Bob the gamekeeper and me found them. I am going to decorate them. I know Mum's the professional but her elbow's a bit sore where Bunjie bit it. A.P.

Monsieur Raymond Levy,
President of Renault Cars,
Paris,
France,
Le Planet

Mardi 28th Mars

Cher Monsieur Raymond Levy,
    Bravo! Felicitations!
    Hearty Congratulations on your decision to fit all Renault cars with anti-pollution catalyst exhaust systems.
    Please export some très vite to Australia where I am going immédiatement.
    Yours sincerely,
    Mademoiselle Anna Pitts
    Age 13 ans

The Old Butcher's,
Leachfield,
Gloucestershire,
England,
The Planet

March 28th

Dear Clare,
I am on my way. On no account post me any
letters to England because I shall be in Australia.
All I have to do is break the news to Auriol that
I cannot be her bridesmaid.

Sorry, it's Wednesday now
I am not at Youth Club.
Sis has just pushed a biro under my door. It is
a single act of friendship in my tragic world.
New Gran has brought Sis back from the hotel.
Sis was throwing up. They brought the last little
piece of the egg with them.
But it is dark chocolate.
Quentin came to work. We decided he had not
noticed it was Sunday. Mum opened the galley to
give him something to do.
Mum said, 'My God!' and sniffed. She fetched
an air spray. Ozone friendly? Don't make me laugh.
Believe it or not, she put me to Quentin-sit. I
could not ring the NSPCC because Mum has
throttled the phone.
Typical Mum.
After two hours, I woke Quentin up and said
wasn't it true that he could manage the gallery by
himself now.

141

He said, 'Yeh.'

I ran out.

I went to Westlow's (whose father will pulverise him) to build our boat with Andrew. Gerald Tappering who has outgrown his strength was waiting there. Also twelve girls from youth Club. So we are a big team. It was drizzling.

We waited one hour and forty minutes in the garden shed. It was quite a squeeze.

A motor bike came.

All the girls ran out.

So did I.

Then I remembered to slow down to a saunter so as to be dead casual.

When he took his crash helmet off, it was not Andrew. It was Kim.

Kim said Andrew was very sorry but he had been held up at his Attendance Centre and could not build a boat today. Then Kim said goodbye.

Kim has softly waving, light brown hair, a square jaw and challenging grey eyes. And when he smiles, it is like Jason Donovan.

None of the girls knew his surname. They said he was not local.

I have carved

on my bedroom wall.

It is a beautiful, short name.

All the girls went home.

Gerald Tappering went to church.

Westlow and me made a boat out of an old door we found in his shed. We tied a rope to the front. Bunjie is going to gallop along the bank pulling us.

Mrs Westlow gave us tea. It was tongue.

Mr Westlow was there. Unfortunately, I had forgotten to ask Westlow if Mr Westlow kept his pulverising in the family or if it spilt over on to his friends.

I ate the tongue.

When I got home, Gerald Tappering was wavering around our gallery. Quentin was asleep. Mum was at a Craft Fayre selling her wares. Bob, the gamekeeper, has gone with her. Is this part of his husband designs?

We poked Quentin awake. He said, 'Yeh,' and went back to sleep. Gerald Tappering said Quentin was a Godsend to shoplifters. He drags God into everything.

He asked me if I fancied Westlow. Quelle crudité. I asked him why he wasn't in church.

He said he had lost his faith. When I enquired how he'd done that, he said God didn't answer his prayers.

I was getting pushed for time with my aniseed balls. I suggested he gave God a little break for a while and took up hunt sabotaging with me. He looked really scared and said his uncle was a huntsman.

He said I would be caught and God would punish me. I said he couldn't have God both ways but just to be on the safe side, why didn't he pray for me to be caught. That way, God wouldn't answer his prayers and it was guaranteed I would walk free.

He said God was no joking matter. I agreed He seemed more on the serious side and went into the kitchen to start work with Mum's rolling pin on the aniseed balls.

After a bit, GT came in and asked if he could sit with me because the smell in the gallery gave him hay fever. Oh, for Brute!

Sis came in and said she was going over to Daisy's with New Gran and Bunjie to get his hair all plaited up for the hunt. The plan was to pretend to Bunjie he was just going out to tea and then sneak up behind and plait him while someone at the front fed him cake.

I wished her luck.

She asked what I was doing. 'Making scent,' I replied. Which was not a mendacious statement.

When she'd gone, Gerald Tappering said didn't I think my little sister was pretty. I said, 'Chacun à son goût,' which is French for not really.

Gerald said didn't we have a food processor because the rate I was grinding, I wouldn't be ready till next hunting season.

To my delight, I remembered the Piranha had one and we shifted the whole outfit to her flat. Would you believe, after the sixtieth bag, the processor gave a sudden groan and stopped working. Gerald Tappering said they didn't make things to last any more.

We took it to pieces to see what was wrong but we couldn't fix it. We went back to hand grinding. Anyway, it was Greener by hand.

Then GT invented a way of hitting the whole bag with the back of the Piranha's Le Creuset iron frying pan. It was fun too because the bag popped like a balloon. But he is so wavery, eventually he missed the bag and caused a crack in the Piranha's ceramic hot plates so we moved to the sitting room because the carpet in there couldn't crack.

At the end, we had three little bags of aniseed powder. It goes to nothing.

We arranged to meet at the Old Butcher's just before dawn. I agreed he would only help carry the bags while I did the scattering so as not to annoy his uncle, the huntsman.

When we went downstairs, New Gran and Sis were back. They said Bunjie was plaited but he'd given New Gran a little nip, and also entirely eliminated Daisy from tomorrow's hunt.

New Gran said really suspiciously, 'And what have you two been up to?'

But when I said, 'Nothing much,' she left it, even though GT went milk-white with fright and bolted off home before I could ask him to tea.

Mum wasn't back from the Craft Fayre. I made tea. I woke Quentin up to see if he wanted any.

He said, 'Yeh.'

When I asked didn't he think he'd mind the gallery better if he didn't go to sleep all the time, he said, 'Yeh, but the smell is so bad in here, going to sleep is the only thing to do to get away from it.'

So he *can* speak!

Gently, I told him the secret of Brute.

Very unfortunately, Quentin has inherited that really loopy look from his father, Mr Bull, which makes you worry he is not all there.

He did not stay for tea.

That night my alarm went off. At first I could not imagine what it thought it was trying to do to

145

me. Then I remembered the hunt. It was 5:30 a.m.

I dressed in the dark and stole downstairs to let Gerald Tappering in. The traitor was not there. I resolved to go it alone. In case he was just late, I left the door on the latch for him.

With the help of Mum's new, improved bike lamp, I found a carrier bag under the Piranha's kitchenette sink. Just as I was putting the bags of aniseed into it, I heard the Piranha's front door open and the light went on in her hall.

That Gerald Tappering, I thought. He hasn't a clue about being a saboteur.

'Don't switch on the light,' I whispered, 'or we'll be caught red handed.'

Quelle erreur!

The front door banged shut and the key turned in the lock and then I heard the Piranha's voice outside screaming blue murder.

I thought I must be having hallucinations of the ears like St Joan of Arc and be in for a life of fame and flame because the Piranha, I knew, was in Turkey and here was I hearing the Piranha screaming that there was a burglar in her flat.

I heard everybody waking up and screaming.

I heard Sis cry.

So I knew then it was for real.

I shouted it was only me but they all stampeded downstairs. I could hear them faintly screaming in the kitchen. Then I heard them thunder upstairs again into my room. I called and called but they only screamed and then down they all went again.

Then a car started up and drove off fast. I bellowed but they were making too much racket downstairs to hear. I tried to phone them on the

Piranha's phone. Thanks to Mum, I could not get through.

I decided to climb out of the window. The Old Butcher's is unexpectedly tall. Even when it's so dark you can hardly see the garden below. I am here (only just) to tell you, the knotted sheet idea you read about in books is a total no-no. Maybe it's different when you have to use the Piranha's broderie anglaise duvet covers. To cut a long story short, the knots come undone.

On landing, I dropped two of my aniseed bags. Hours of work wasted. I hid the other one and limped round to the back door to give that Piranha a piece of my mind for locking me in.

Mum rushed at me and hugged me and shouted, 'Are you all right? Are you all right?' As for the Piranha, she looked amazingly untidy and very white for one just back from sunnier climes. She was wearing her dark glasses still though.

Not a sign of Sis and New Gran.

I said no, I was not all right and that the Piranha had locked me in her flat. Mum claims now I called the Piranha a delirious old dragon. But you know Mum.

The police came.

New Gran and Sis came back from Bamford where they'd driven to telephone the police. Which was hard for New Gran because of the little nip Bunjie had given her at his plaiting tea party.

We all had tea.

The police said it was lucky we weren't a bigger family or they would never have any time left at all to catch the real criminals.

It seems, when my family found my bed empty, they thought the burglar in the Piranha's flat had taken me hostage. We all chuckled over the mistake and then the police went.

And my family turned into a plague of demons. New Gran turned into Super Demon. United, they screamed. At me.

It was dawn. My chances of sabotaging the hunt were shrinking. Soothingly, I suggested they all went back to bed for a nap.

For some reason, that really seemed to irritate them. Mega scream.

I said I was only thinking of them. Jeering laughter. Ah, well. They will appreciate me when I have gone down under.

It was broad daylight before they all stamped off to get dressed. Next thing, there were horrible howls from the Piranha's flat. My new-grown hair stood on end. We all ran to see what was up.

The Piranha was raving that her flat had been vandalised. I have to admit, it did look a little messy.

New Gran said, 'See what I mean.' (Recurring.)

Mum asked what I thought I'd been doing.

I said, 'Nothing much.'

Then they all started repeating 'nothing much', like it was a competition to see how many different ways you could say, 'nothing much'.

Mum booked me for a serious talk in an hour's time and ran a bath for the Piranha. It turns out the Piranha has been in a Turkish prison for two days. She was really ratty because she could not get through to us on our telephone to come and rescue her so eventually, she rescued herself.

James, the chauffeur, is still in prison. He

punched a young Turkish friend of the Piranha's who wanted to be her toy boy. There are lots of good things about my grandmother but I am sorry to say that some people will do anything for money.

As Mum and the Piranha were having a go about the phone, I took the opportunity to leave. I went to let Ethel out. But she was dead.

In my excitement about sabotaging the hunt, I had forgotten to put her safely to bed. A fox had bitten her head off and left it and some of her feathers in the garden.

It did not seem very fair. Perhaps if the fox had known I was trying to save its life it would have spared Ethel's. I cannot believe it but I will never, never see her again.

New Gran came scooting round the corner of the house with my last bag of aniseed. 'What's this?' She was v. breathless.

'Aniseed powder.'

'Oh, is it,' she said. 'Don't think you can throw the wool in my eyes.' She really said that. It made me sort of smile, even though I was holding Ethel's head and my throat was aching.

'I know what this is,' she said, like she expected a gold star for knowing – which was strange because I had just told her what it was. I asked her to fetch Mum.

'With pleasure,' she said.

Mum and me and Sis buried the head and feathers with full rites.

We cried.

Bob, the gamekeeper came round to say it was his fault. He'd been so busy with Mum at the Fayre, it had slipped his mind to come and help put Ethel to bed. But I knew it was my fault.

Everyone was kind.

It only lasted a minute.

Mr Bull the reporter came to say his lad was really, really upset because I'd said Quentin had B.O. and Mrs Sally Bull, Mr Bull's ex-wife, was spitting nails.

I explained how Quentin had made the gallery smell and how he had uttered a Cry for Help.

Everyone streamed off to smell the gallery. They found the cause. They came streaming back with it.

I'd forgotten about the eel I'd hidden from Mum.

Quelle pong!

Bob was really cross Mum had never received his gift. Then New Gran put her oar in and dangled my bag of aniseed which was hard for her because of Bunjie's little nip. She said I was a purveyor of drugs. I said didn't she mean a pusher.

New Gran shuddered and said in a mega whisper, 'See what I mean?' She dropped the aniseed bag like it was burning her fingers. It fell with a plop on the rotten eel. 'Crack!' breathed New Gran.

Things were looking dead serious so I came clean about the sabotage plan. You'd expect, wouldn't you, they'd be overjoyed I was not a junkie?

I sometimes think the amount people scream could put my hearing at risk. The noise was a bit reduced when the Piranha pushed her head out of her bathroom window and bawled merrily, 'Hello, Phil,' and Mr Bull gave a little skip and ran off to visit the Piranha.

I was feeling v. low about Ethel and said I was going to bed. New Gran said, 'Is that child going to get away with all this?'

Mum asked New Gran whose daughter I was. Which was rather hurtful. I had not realised Mum is that absent-minded. I hope she is not catching Alzheimer's disease already. Anyway, her lapse of memory really got up New Gran's nose. The row disturbed my sleep.

Typical Mum.

Later, Mum woke me with a cup of tea and gave me a serious talk about RIGHT and WRONG. I can't remember the details but Ethel's head being bitten off is neither. It is Nature.

RIGHT is hunting, and also buying the Piranha a new food processor with my organic wages, and washing the flower bed mud out of her duvet covers and cleaning up her carpet in my free time, and writing an apology to Quentin, and replacing the Piranha's bottle of brandy.

Also missing Youth Club for two weeks is RIGHT, and I expect if I'd mentioned to Mum the aniseed balls were on her paper bill, paying back for those would be RIGHT as well.

I made a snap decision to let sleeping dogs lie.

In a nutshell, RIGHT is working you chilblains to the bone and then spending all your wages on luxuries for your grandmother, writing to people who probably can't read, missing the charity boat race and beating up foxes.

Mum did not linger long over WRONG. It is borrowing things and stopping people beating up foxes.

Basically, RIGHT is what other people do and WRONG is what you do.

Sis came and thanked me for making her miss the hunt. She said hunting may be RIGHT but it is ***ing painful. I told her not to swear. She said, 'What's wrong with swearing?'

I checked over Mum's list of RIGHT and WRONG.

'Nothing,' I said.

We made a wreath for Ethel's grave.

Bunjie kicked my knee cap so now I am limping on both legs. He is probably angry with me for making him miss the hunt so he couldn't go A.W.O.L.

As everyone is v. angry with me and the hunting season is over, I shall clear up my affairs tomorrow morning and set out for Heathrow with Gainsborough and a heavy heart in the afternoon.

With love from your friend in England,

Anna Pitts

P.S. Sis has just pushed a note under my door. (It is not that I'm sulking I am just keeping to my room.) The note says Kim's surname is Vanguisingham-Browne.

Life is cruel. A.P.

P.P.S. Just think, by the time you get this letter, I shall be living with you and Mr and Mrs Hannock in Australia. A.P.

P.P.P.S. Also, I shall have departed before the dentist can fit the brace he is making for my teeth and Mum gets her paper bill. A.P.

152

To:-
Quentin Bull,
c/o Mrs Sally Bull,
29, Landsgate Crescent,
Swanton,
Gloucestershire,
England,
The Planet

You can't bring back the magic carpet BETTER BUY A RENAULT

March 29th

Dear Quentin,
I am sorry I said you smelt. It was an eel.
Please come back and work for Mum. It is all right. I shall not be here.
Have you many experiences of Mr Bull as a dad? Perhaps you would care to share them with me as I have an interest.
Yours sincerely,
Anna Pitts
P.S. I know you cannot afford a Renault or any form of car so don't worry. A.P.

The Old Butcher's,
Leachfield,
Gloucestershire,
England,
The Planet

SO WOT?

Friday, April 21st

Dear Clare,
I am B cup! Tara! Well, there is a bit of room

153

to spare but I am definitely not A any more. Say B minus. Still haven't started yet. I go and look every morning at break. The Bible says, 'Seek and ye shall find.' It is wrong.

I asked Mum to send me to a gynaecologist.

She said no.

Sorry I didn't come to Australia. Please go ahead and send your letters here now I am still here and not there. I had to make the supreme sacrifice.

Remember when we were young, a cabinet minister said all the British eggs were rotten and everybody else said no they aren't and so she gave up being a cabinet minister and then they found that all the British eggs were rotten? Well, it was this stuff called Salmonella.

Sis thought Salmonella was a Fish Princess but it isn't. It makes killer eggs.

Now it's got into the chicken farmer's eggs so he can't sell them to his customers because it would be murder and he's put all his hens to death. And he doesn't have any money so his wife, who looks like a model, cancelled Mum's commission.

And Mum went into deep space.

I made her so many cups of coffee we ran out and could not afford to buy any more. I thought of borrowing some from the Piranha's flat because she is away on her honeymoon but I've been caught like that before.

Gainsborough and me were all packed. We really, really needed to get away to Australia. We sat by Ethel's grave. We were wracked by desire to live in Narrowmine. It rained. We went in.

Mum was phoning round all the banks. She was

154

holding the line to speak to her fourth bank manager to ask him for a loan.

She said, 'Don't worry, Anna.'

'Because I am the eldest,' I said, 'I am staying here with you.'

'No, you mustn't miss school,' she said, 'I'll run you in.'

So I don't think she heard me. Then the bank manager came on the line. He said there was nothing doing.

We moved on to tea.

Naturellement, Shereen has lost her job with the chicken farmer. She is v. bitter because she is running out of cruelty free make-up and we are bridesmaids tomorrow.

We are the chief ones. Shereen's twin cousins all the way from Worcester are the others and there is a little page boy in apricot breeches and coffee tights who is not family.

My apricot bodice with coffee trimmings has had to be let out! For what Auriol calls my 'knockers.' It is très belle. But not so much like a soup tureen.

Quentin has lost his job sleeping in our gallery because we cannot afford to feed him. Nobody comes in. Ever.

I am the only bread-winner, working for Will and Belinda at the organic garden. Principles pay! Which is a veritable jape as I have lost my faith and do not bother with the planet any more.

Bob, the gamekeeper, has just been in with a box

155

of wine for Mum and him. He asked me didn't I miss my little sister now she was away at school. I said 'Yes,' but I kept my fingers crossed behind my back.

To be on the safe side, I added, 'And no.'

And kept them crossed.

Bob has definite husband designs on Mum. I keep trying to picture life with him as a step dad. After an everlasting Yorkie bar, it goes hazy.

I fear we will grow so poor, Mum will marry for money. I asked Quentin how Mr Bull the reporter rated as a dad before he left Mrs Sally Bull whose cheques do not bounce.

He said, 'Ok.'

Then I asked if he could write his name – Quentin.

He gave me the Bull Family Loopy Look. Then he said, 'Yeh.'

I'd asked him because I wanted him to sign my petition to Save the Planet. He said, 'Who are we saving it for?'

I replied kindly, 'People.'

'Why should people have the planet?' Quentin said. 'What's so special about people?'

Have you ever done that thing of opening your mouth to speak and then no words come out? It is like being brain dead. Also it is called gob-smacked. I could not think of why people should have the planet. Can you?

No. You see?

It's just because you've got used to them having it that you think they should.

Then Quentin told me, at the pace people were going, they would soon make the planet uninhabitable for humans and most other things. Something will survive, he told me, but it certainly wouldn't be people and personally he backed genetically engineered tomatoes as being the species most likely to make it.

'So cheer up and stop worrying,' Quentin said. 'Join the party. Get in there and screw up the planet along with everybody else.'

So, I am a born-again polluter. It is much easier except Mum keeps forgetting and leaving me pasta in the oven while she goes to the doctor's.

Butch Hills decided to produce *Arable Agony*, without me but Mrs Jackson, the new music teacher, has told him to write proper tunes for all the lyrics and Butch has to stay late every afternoon la-la-la-ing while she plonks away on the piano. He is v. hoarse and does not speak much. Phew! Phew!

Miss Lane, our ex-music teacher, has gone to be a teacher in Australia. Isn't that a coincidence? So look out for her.

I have left you the script of *Deadly Nitrates* in my will but if you take my advice, you will become a born again polluter. It is v. carefree.

E.g. when there is a disaster like a mega oil leak, even though you feel really sorry for the polar bears and gulls and seaweed etc. while the news is on, and you have to turn off the pictures of them dying because you can't look, you just go and play records and think how quiet the world will be when it is covered in these big, fat tomatoes and that is all there is to it.

Must stop soon and go to rehearsal for Auriol's wedding. With the Piranha's we didn't bother. The

Piranha wore white for virginity. Is that what is meant by a white lie? Ho, ho.

New Gran also wore white.

Sadly, she missed the ceremony because quite by accident, the Piranha gave her the wrong directions and poor old New Gran landed up at the cattle market.

The rest of us made it to the registry office. But I don't rate it. The Piranha and Mr Bull were in and out in a flash but the tea was good.

Now they have gone to Turkey for a honeymoon. They plan to stay with some of the Piranha's old friends from prison and to visit James the chauffeur who is still banged up in Istanbul.

I don't have much hope of Mr Bull as a grandfather. He does not seem to know the rules. At the wedding feast, I told him what date my birthday was and he just did his loopy look so I wrote it on my serviette for him. Later he blew his nose in it. The prospects are lousy.

And rather dead boring.

Bob, the gamekeeper, said weddings were catching and gave Mum a hug, and a shoulder of venison, and a Yorkie bar for me. I said I was on a diet.

Mum has just phoned to say –

(a) she's got a puncture.

(b) to fetch Bunjie – which means she's forgotten my wedding rehearsal. The way Mum carries on you'd think I had no social life at all, and

(c) not to wait up for her.

I tried phoning Sis at the castle school but she is in something called prep.

With love from your friend in England,

Anna Pitts

P.S. I will send you a photo of me in my apricot bridesmaid dress with coffee trimmings. Also we have coffee shoes and coffee wreaths in our hair. I am really, really looking forward to it and if I do not smile, my brace will not show in the least bit.

P.P.S. I have bought some très spesh dark blue kohl to match my eyes. It was reduced to clear in Boots and just right. I have been doing application practice. At first, I kept crashing Kohl into my glasses but now, I hold them a few centimetres away from my nose so I can still look, but I hit my lids instead. I hope your letters get here soon. It is very quiet here at the Old Butcher's and rather dead boring. A.P.

The Old Butcher's,
Leachfield,
Gloucestershire,
England,
The Planet

Friday, May 12th

Dear Clare,

Would you believe, we are so ruined, Mum has
taken a part-time art teaching job at Sis's castle
school even though the school is against her beliefs.

It is strange how my principles bring in £4 a week
and Mum's non-principles make her £140. So
principles don't pay after all and it is a good thing
I have given them up.

The night before Auriol's wedding, Bunjie tried
to bite my eyebrow and broke the left lens of my
glasses. I told him how ponies along with people
were dying out and soon it would be all tomatoes
silently rotting. He had a second try.

Next morning, I had a huge black eye. Bob, the
gamekeeper, said it looked like I'd been two rounds
with Mike Tyson.

I could have died.

Mum was no help as she was in the bathroom
with a bug. I took her a cup of tea and asked her
to swap bathrooms because hers had the best mirror.
She just moaned. I found the tea two days later,
cold and scummy.

I put one layer of Tea Rose foundation on. And
then I put a layer and a layer and a layer and a layer
and a layer of it on my black eye. After that, I went
ahead as normal except I finished off with a slightly

more than light dusting of this really ace white powder with shimmery flakes in it.

The blue kohl was un peu tricky partly because I could only look through half my broken glasses and partly because my left eye was rather small and lumpy. But once I'd got it on, you certainly wouldn't have known I'd been bitten in the eyebrow.

As I was leaving for Shereen's to put on my bridesmaid's gear, I met New Gran who has come down to get Sis out of the castle and take her to the wedding. She said, 'My God! What have you done to your eye?'

I went up to the Piranha's flat and borrowed her spare pair of shades. I popped them on as we went into the church so my eye would be unnoticeable. It became v. dark.

For that reason, although I swept down the aisle like I was in Mum's dressing gown and had not missed the rehearsal at all, I did not spot when Auriol, at the head of the procession, had stopped, and I ran into the twin bridesmaid from Worcester ahead of me who went into the little page boy ahead of her who went into Auriol who fell on to the vicar and it is all on video except there is a break where the vicar fell back on to the man making the video.

I could have died.

Later, at the feast down at the football club room, Mr Westlow, who will pulverise his son, said it was the best laugh he'd had in years and to take Bunjie to the knacker's yard.

I have looked up knacker's yard in the dictionary. It is a killing field for old ponies.

As it will all be giant tomatoes soon, it did not seem fair to him to jump the gun.

Later still, Gerald Tappering tried to kiss me. Later still, Robin Westlow succeeded so perhaps I should always wear blue kohl.

With love from your friend in England,
Anna Pitts

P.S. I have found out Kim Vanguisingham-Browne lives in Belgium. His dad is on the EEC. Also you can get day trips. A.P.

P.P.S. I had not realised you could really miss kissing. A.P.

The Old Butcher's,
Leachfield,
Gloucestershire,
England,
The Planet

Saturday May 13th

Dear Clare,

The Piranha is back. Mr Bull, the reporter, is a wash out as a grandfather. Yesterday, he forgot my name. Quentin must have v. low standards of parenting.

Mum is still lying about with her bug. I asked her what my dad the art student's surname is. She said, 'What a time to ask.' Then she retched, then she said, 'Smith.'

Sis's friend, Daisy, worked out on her computer at the castle there are four and a half million John

Smiths living in the world excluding China so I do not rate my chances of finding him before we all turn into tomatoes.

Sorry, it's Wednesday 17th now

Westlow and me have kissed again. And more. When my brace is off we are going to try the other way that originated in France.

He is better at kissing than Baz Goodbody was. I am suspicious he has had practice which makes me un peu furious but he says he has not.

He asked me if I had and I said, no. Avec les doigts comme ça

It seems a shame it will be all tomatoes soon and no more kissing even if it is a waste of lipstick.

Remember Anita The Great, from our old school? Well, she is coming to stay next Bank Holiday.

With love from your friend in England,
Anna Pitts

P.S. What is Australian kissing like? Does every country have its own variety of kiss? A.P.

Old Butcher's,
Leachfield,
Gloucestershire,
England,
The Planet

Friday May 19th

Dear Clare,
   TARA!!! The Bible does not lie. But it was not at break. It was at 8:03 p.m. Mum's lent me all the equipment. Tomorrow, I go out and buy my very own.
   Mum hugged me and upped my pocket money to cover the cost.
   Well, she gave me an I.O.U.
   Mum was a bit snuffly so I hope she has not hugged her bug on to me. She called me her little girl, which is mendacious because now we are equals, and she said not to use tampons at my stage. Quelle crudité!

Sorry, it's Saturday 20th now
   The Piranha has thrown Mr Bull out.
   Would you believe! It turns out Mum's bug is not a bug, it is a baby. It is coming later. I am really, really pleased and pray it will not have a runny nose like Dan at the organic garden.
   The Piranha says it is Mr Bull's baby and has given him the push.
   Quelle row!
   So I have lost a grandfather and gained a sister/brother.
   Bob, the gamekeeper, broke the kitchen table in

half with his fist and strode off home because it isn't his baby.

New Gran, who is down for the weekend to take Sis out to lunch, rushed to the shops and bought it three little suits. They are really stylish.

Sis refuses to come home from the castle.

At the moment, Mr Bull is bashing tempestuously on the Piranha's new front door out in the street and shouting really personal stuff like 'Please, please, Piggsy Wiggsy.'

He is a broken man.

Also he does not realise that the Piranha came down here half an hour ago for some lemon for her gin and tonic and a serious talk with Mum. We are too poor for lemons. The s. talk is happening in Mum's bedroom which is furthest away from the noise Mr Bull is creating.

New Gran is on the phone pleading with Sis to come home but she won't because she is not going to be the youngest any more.

Mum has just come in for the calendar.

She made me a bottle for my stomach ache.

9:30 p.m.

There was this really big row. Cape Canaveral eat your heart out!

Mr Bull stopped attacking the Piranha's front door and there was this lovely silence. You could just hear Mum and the Piranha exchanging views in the bedroom.

Minutes later, Mr Bull stormed the house with the doctor in tow. The doctor was très angry because Mr Bull had snatched him out of surgery rather roughly. Everyone gathered furiously round the broken kitchen table.

But the doctor said again and again that Mum's baby wasn't his. Mr Bull shouted, 'Prove it.'

'If you must know, I've had a vasectomy,' the doctor said.

Mr Bull cried.

I could not bear to tear myself away to fetch my dictionary because by then Mr Bull was lying on the kitchen floor and beating it with his fists. But as vasectomy is to do with sex, Mum kindly explained it to me while the doctor and New Gran tried to pick Mr Bull up and the Piranha filled her empty glass from the tap and poured it over him for hysterics, she said.

Vasectomy is getting fixed so you are not a eunuch but everlasting babyless.

I was amazed to hear it because I'd had my money on it being the doctor. Well, money in theory.

I think Mum must have spoken up for Mr Bull in the bedroom because the Piranha led him away for a gin.

The doctor asked rather stonily, 'Who's the lucky man then?' Mum smiled. And he sighed and he went away.

I reckon when it comes to a dad, my sister/brother is going to get about as far as I have with John Smith, the art student.

New Gran said, 'Well, well, well, well,' in a joke voice, and raced off to buy another kitchen table and a pram.

And I thought what a pity it was that my baby sister/brother is going to be pushed out by the tomatoes. I went and played records for hours to cure myself of the thought. But it did not work.

My stomach ache came back. Also Sis, with the castle's matron. They want to close it for the weekend.

Mum had a serious talk with us and said the new baby she was going to have was a product of Great Love. Sis asked if it would come with a built-in grandmother of its own.

I rang Quentin for advice this afternoon because it is impossible to stay cheerful about my baby sister/brother and the tomato takeover but Mrs Sally Bull, Mr Bull's ex wife, said Quentin was asleep.

I asked her to take a message for him to say I am absolutely not tomatoist (you know they are my favourite sandwich, except with cheese – yuk! yuk!) but I could not see why tomatoes should have the planet all to themselves. Just like he could not see why people should. And didn't he know someone who would stick up for the other things like the fish and tigers and babies and celery, etc?

'And,' asked Mrs S.B., strangely testily, 'the spineless, slimy, lowdown, old creeps too?' I agreed Slugs' Rights were also v. important.

She said she would give Quentin the message the minute he woke up which would probably be some time next week.

Clare, answer me this. If you are a born-again person can you get un-born? Or would that make you not exist at all?

There is only one way to find out. Quake! Quake!

With love from your friend in England,
Anna Pitts

P.S. We have searched high and low but all three

of the new little baby suits have vanished. Quelle mystery. A.P.

P.P.S. New Gran has found them. Sis is in the dog house. A.P.

To:-
The Secretary General,
United Nations,
New York,
NY1017,
USA,
The Planet

May 29th

Dear Secretary General,

As you are on hob-nobbing terms with all the Leaders of the World, I am sending my Plan to you first.

It will arrive the day after this as I have to go into Swanton to get it photocopied for you tomorrow. So that is something to look forward to, isn't it?

The Plan will save the Planet from genetically engineered tomatoes etc. and keep it beautiful for all, from smallest to gynormous.

It is a simple, step-by-step, easy to follow blueprint for a future. Please make sure every Leader has a copy placed on his/her desk and insist

168

in a firm but friendly fashion they *read* it and don't just look at the pictures.

Also, tell them to stop running the Planet like it is one big Closing Down Sale.

Tell them to do it soon.

Yours sincerely,
Anna Pitts
Age 13 years

The Old Butcher's
Leachfield,
Gloucestershire,
England,
The Planet

Bank Holiday Monday May 29th
Half Term!!

Dear Clare,

Anita the Great's brother said when he brought her down here that he will take us both on a trip to Brussels in Belgium. Ooh la la! Watch this space.

Tomorrow, Anita and me are going into town to get my Plan to Save the Planet photocopied for the Secretary General of the United Nations.

Would you believe? She is C cup now! Do you measure in cups in Australia? Sis said it is more likely to be in billabongs. Sometimes I think Sis's jokes will drive me into intensive care.

On our way to Will and Belinda's with Bunjie's dung, Anita the G. and me met Butch Hills with the face like a bowl of muesli and she staged a counter hi-jack of my musical, *Arable Agony*.

Butch agreed to all her terms like lightning. Also that I am to be the new character I have added – The Genii of the Genes – who is entrapped in a test tube. But I get out and dance a sinewy dance so I must keep in with Sis. Butch told Anita that it was just fine by him.

I am thinking of asking the Piranha and Mr Bull, my grandfather for a chest expander for my birthday.

Gerald Tappering, who has outgrown his strength, has asked Anita to the disco. He asked Sis first but Sis said no.

Sis is v. gloomy about Mum's baby. She says it is ok for me because I will always be the eldest whatever happens but she has been assassinated as the youngest. I said she meant superseded and she said no assassinated, and just because I wore STs it did not make me Brain of Britain.

Anita the G. and me put a load of blusher on her to cheer her up and she rode off on Bunjie. But he got away from her. We rang the police.

Sis is on the h.w. bottle again.

Would you believe? Mum had begun stencilling a little bed thing ready for the new baby (it is called a cradle and looks really old fashioned and unhygienic) and an American lady came in and ordered twenty for her show room in New York and now a magazine is going to photograph them too.

Auriol is buying one as well. Hers has to be ready by two and a half weeks today. So that is why Mr Westlow said when I accidentally knocked Auriol over at her wedding that it was the best position for a fallen woman to get hitched in.

Mr Westlow does not seem to know that Mrs Westlow has ordered a cradle too. Also Shereen's mum has and Mrs Jackson the new music teacher so it looks like Mum has hit the jackpot with her baby and it is not so much weddings that are catching as babies.

Butch Hills has just rung up. He asked Anita the Great to go to the disco with him. And guess what she said.

I am sending you a photocopy of my Plan to Save the Planet as well as to the Secretary General. Anita the Great says it is ace and will do the trick.

She told me she has been so worried about the planet, she has applied for Child Psychoanalysis but with the state of the National Health, she thought the planet would be over by the time she got it. But now, thanks to The Plan, she has bounced back.

Tomorrow, when we go photocopying, we are going to get Sis's ears pierced too (in deadly secret or New Gran will go comatosed) because all the castle school girls are pierced and are catty about Sis's lobes.

I reckon if we decorate Sis's ears up to maximum load, it will disguise the fact that there is nothing much in between them.

Anita the Great has just said Baz Goodbody received a Christmas card from you last Christmas. Also an Easter and a birthday card and a letter last week so why on ea

The Old Butcher's Gallery,
Leachfield,
Glos

2nd Sept

Dear Clare,
   I found this letter to you from Anna lying about
so I posted it for her. Hope she hasn't kept you wait-
ing for it too long – but you know what she's like.
   Love to your mum and dad and you, of course,
   Ms Pitts